Death on Blackwater Bay

~~ A Novel ~~

Sylvia Melvin

This is a work of fiction. Names, character, places and events are products of the author's imagination and are used fictitiously. Any resemblance to actual persons, living or dead, locales or events is entirely coincidental.

Email: **sallymelvin6053@gmail.com**
Website: **www.sylviamelvin.com**
Blog: **http://sylviasscribbles.blogspot.com**

© 2013 Sylvia Melvin
ISBN –139781491017968
ISBN-1491017961

Also by Sylvia Melvin

Mystery:
Death Behind the Dunes
Death Beyond the Breakers
Death On Blackwater Bay

Romance:
Summer Guest

Biography:
Helena: Unwavering Courage
Southern Sage: The Honorable Woodrow Melvin

I hope you have a relaxing summer with time to read.
Sincerely,
Sylvia (Sally) Melvin

Acknowledgements

Writing a series of mystery books is not unlike raising a family. The author guides their personalities, becomes attached to each one, and then the time comes to let them go. Many thanks to the following individuals who have supported my journey in writing this book:

~ Judge Robert Hilliard , County Judge
~ Adrianna Spain, Attorney
~ Major Steve Collier, Santa Rosa County Sheriff's Office
~ Richard Subasavage, Assistant Warden, Blackwater River Correctional Facility
~ David Noran, Corvette Connoisseur
~ Stephen Wise, author, editor, and movie producer
~ Albert Melvin, cover photographer and supportive husband
~ The Panhandle Writer's Group

Thank you,

Sylvia Melvin

Chapter One

The slam of metal on metal and the click of the lock turning to secure the doors of the Santa Rosa Prison behind him sent a nauseous chill through Otis Washington's body. Even though he was now a free man and had served his time, that sound would haunt him for the rest of his life. Eighteen years ago he heard it for the first time and it meant one thing—he was a prisoner, a condemned man, found guilty of carjacking and killing an innocent child.

Except it wasn't true. He went to prison an innocent victim of mistaken identity. Never will he forget the face of the judge who sealed his fate. Rage and thoughts of revenge burned within him to the depths of his weary soul and one tormented thought refused to stay behind in that claustrophobic cell. *Someone will pay.*

Otis ran his long black fingers through sweat-soaked corkscrew sprigs of graying hair. A stream of perspiration trickled down the sides of a misshapen nose and accentuated a glistening scar across his right cheekbone. Life in prison shored him up for the unexpected.

The warmth of the early March sun felt good, and though the warden had given him the state required sum of fifty dollars, Otis decided to walk the three miles to town rather than spend much needed money on a bus or taxi. Besides, he wanted to see what changes he'd missed over the years. As his eyes surveyed the landscape, he noted new businesses, fast food establishments, and an elementary school buzzing with outdoor recess activity. The innocent laughter of children caused him to stop and listen. The laughter lingered in his ears—almost like a long lost melody. After twenty minutes of walking, a familiar sight caught his attention. Several logging trucks carrying yellow and longleaf pine sped by headed for the pulp and paper mill.

No change there, mused Otis. Not used to the constant radiant heat, he removed the jacket provided by the state and slung it over his right shoulder. A slight hunch in his back suggested a weary, defeated man weighed down by depression and resentment—burdened by life. Although, he was a middle-aged man of fifty-three, his appearance and gait made him look much older.

The construction of a new intersection confused him and Otis looked at the sun to get his bearings. He needed to go west toward the Blackwater Bay. Back to his home, assuming it was still there after a couple of severe hurricanes that ravaged the area. It wasn't much of a place—a Southern style fish camp—but it gave him a livelihood, and here he spent the best years of his life by his beloved bay. He'd never forgotten the look of the water, the stench of rotting fish guts, and the buzz of flying insects that inhabited the shoreline grasses. Otis turned left and immediately recognized a beer joint he'd occasionally patronized.

A smirk crossed his face as he recalled the past. *Oh, yes, I recall being thrown out of there more than once. Mainly for fighting—with Owen. Twins don't always see eye to eye.* A flood of childhood memories surfaced and he could visualize his mama shaking her head and lamenting, "They's as different as Cain and Able. One's the good seed and the other the bad. Breaks my heart."

Like bitter bile, the thought of his brother caused Otis to spit on the side of the road as though he could rid himself of his despised kin. Not once in eighteen years did Owen come to the prison to visit him.

The closer Otis got to the Blackwater, the more a nervous excitement stirred in the pit of his stomach. For the first time all day, his spirit lifted and his feet trod faster than usual. Without warning, a black cloud threatened to dampen his hopes. *What if the camp's gone? Where will I go?*

As suddenly as the negative thought came, it quickly dissipated the moment Otis saw the weather-beaten remains of his house. To Otis, it looked like a mansion. True, the roof needed new shingles, and a coat of paint on the peeling exterior walls and porch would do wonders, but this land and battered old building was his only possession on earth. Never was Otis more grateful to his father than at this moment. *Thank you, Big Daddy. You willed this to me 'cause you knew I'd be the one who'd appreciate it. I promise you'll be proud of it again.*

Before going in, Otis walked the property line. His feet trampled down the overgrown weeds and underbrush while fine white sand crunched beneath his shoes. A *good bushhoggin' is all it needs. Gotta make it look decent around here for business. Wonder if I still have a boat? Lucky if it ain't bin stole.*

With that thought in mind, Otis went in search of his jon boat. He knew that not only was a boat required should someone want to rent it, but he needed it to catch fish. To his surprise, he located one under a lean-to where a moldy tarpaulin shielded it from the elements. Elated, he pulled off the cover and yanked and tugged on the bow until he could maneuver his craft down to the water.

"Hmm," mused Otis as he looked at the boat launch area. "Tire tracks and footprints. Looks as though some folks been trespassin'. Oh, well, I'll put a stop to that."

Satisfied his boat was tied securely, he walked to the camp and, out of habit, tried the door. It opened. Puzzled, Otis clearly remembered locking the place up and leaving the key with his Aunt Lucy. Once inside, he looked around and discovered signs of habitation. Dirty cups and dozens of beer bottles littered the cupboards. A pair of rubber boots sat beside the wood burning stove and rumpled blankets hung off the side of a camping cot.

Suspicious that his brother was the unwelcome invader, seething angry thoughts beat against his temples. *Oh, no, brother, eighteen innocent years behind bars will not soon be forgotten.*

Chapter Two

Otis woke with a start. Why was the sun blaring in an uncovered window? It was too high in the sky for sunrise. The silence spooked him—no slamming cell doors, no cussing, no roll call. Completely disoriented, he shook his head and rubbed crusted sleep deposits from the corners of his eyes.

Slowly, he began to recognize objects in the room. Fishing rods of different sizes and types leaned against one wall, nets hung on nails, bait buckets were stacked two feet high. An outboard motor lay on the floor where it had leaked oil and gasoline, leaving a circular stain. Familiarity took root in Otis's mind and he realized this was home.

Peace settled over his shaking body, still clad in the clothes given to him by the warden. Hunger gnawed in the pit of his stomach. *A plate of grits and eggs would sure taste good this mornin'. Don't s'pose a fella could find a can of coffee bin layin' around all these years.* The low growl of his empty stomach urged him off the cot and sent him searching through the cupboards for any kind of rations.

On the second shelf, he spotted canned beans, soup, a box of crackers torn open and nibbled on by some rodent that had invaded the larder, and the one item that put a smile on Otis's face—Community Coffee. He grabbed the can and held it to his nose. He could imagine the deep roasted aroma and satisfying initial gulp sliding down his throat. First, though, he needed to build a fire in the cook stove and boil some water. This simple task brought satisfaction, and before long bubbling amber liquid gurgled in a dented percolator.

For the next three or four hours, Otis used his time cleaning up the camp, and with each task completed, he felt a sense of accomplishment. As he surveyed his work, he mused, *Gotta get the word out that Camp Blackwater is open for business again.* He fingered the bills in his pocket. *This here money ain't gonna go far, but I need food and fish bait. Maybe I can hitch a ride into town.*

Luck would have it that the first vehicle to stop and pick him up was a distant cousin.

"Hey, man, that you, Otis?" exclaimed the driver. "When you get out?"

Otis, just as surprised to see kin, offered Tyrone his hand. "Yesterday. I'm on my way to town for some grub and bait."

"You gonna open the camp again? I hope so. Folks bin missin' you over there."

"Spread the word, cuz. I'm back in business. Tell me what's happenin' with our folks? Who's died, married, moved on, you know?"

Tyronne glanced at Otis and with hesitation in his voice began, "We-l-l, I hear Owen's livin' with some woman over in Pensacola."

At the mention of his brother's name, a hard grimace took the softness from Otis's face and Tyronne tried to recover the camaraderie between them by chuckling, "Course he always had an eye for the women."

The look Otis gave Tyronne caused him to change the subject. "Ole Uncle Cleetis died three, four years ago with pneumonia. Aunt Bessie's never been the same. Lawd, how that woman could sing. Take the roof right off the church and straight to heaven." A wistful smile broke over Tyronne's shining face. "Hey, Otis, you gonna come back to church, ain't cha? Your mama would be so proud."

"Don't be lookin' for me too soon," replied Otis. "I need some time to settle back in. I reckon my faith's slipped a bit the past eighteen years. Me and the Man up there," Otis raised his head and rolled his eyes upward, "we got some talkin' to do."

"I get ya." Tyronne dropped the subject as he slowed down and wheeled his vehicle into a parking lot. "Otis, this here is called a grocery outlet store. Things is supposed to be cheaper, but you'd never know it by me with five growing kids and another on the way." Tyronne shook his head from side to side and confessed, "If I'd knowed that wife of mine was so fertile, I might never had married her. But as the Good Book tells us, 'blessed is the man with many arrows in his quiver.'"

Otis laughed out loud. The sound of his own voice responding in amusement felt strange. "Tyronne, by the time you're done, they'll be ten sittin' around your table. I recall you got yourself one good lookin' woman."

"Lawdy me!" responded Tyronne as he slapped Otis on the back. "One thing for sure—you still got your sense of humor."

The two cousins hung out together as Otis completed his errands. At the Goodwill Store, he found another pair of jeans, a couple tee-shirts, a pair of used Crocs, and some underwear and socks.

"Sure feels good to be out of those prison garbs. If I never see sky blue again, it won't be any loss to me. I never felt comfortable in 'em. Loose fittin' and looked like those scrubs doctors wear."

Tyronne took notice that Otis used all but fifty cents of his allotted money, and from the growling in his cousin's stomach it, was obvious his kin had not eaten any breakfast. Without asking, he maneuvered his truck into a lot beside the Waffle House.

"This one's on me, cuz. Welcome home."

"Mighty grateful. I promise there'll be flounder on your table before the week's out."

"Deal," shouted Tyronne. "C'mon, I can smell the grits and sausage gravy from here."

* * *

By late afternoon, Otis was ready to flounder. A three-prong gig, on an eight-foot pole, a rigged-up light consisting of a twelve-volt battery, a hundred-watt light bulb, and a metal circular shield lay on one of the boat seats. In the bow was an empty cooler ready to receive the catch. Beneath his seat, Otis placed a twelve-gauge shotgun he'd hidden under the floorboards of his house in years past.

Itching to get out on the water, Otis untied the boat and had one leg over the side ready to jump in the craft when the sound of crunching sand stopped him. He looked toward the road and saw a vehicle towing a boat trailer into the launch area.

Changing his mind, he re-tied his boat, picked up his gun, and walked up to the car.

"This here's private property, fellas. I run a fish camp, and it'll cost you ten bucks to park and put your boat in."

A look of surprise registered on the driver's face. "Since when ole man? I've been coming down here for years. Never cost me a dime. Ain't seen you before."

"Been away a while, but I'm back and you're my first customer today."

One of the passengers opened a back door and started to object. "Like he—"

Before he could finish his profanity, the click of the hammer on Otis's shotgun stopped him cold.

The driver settled the issue. With a rev of the car engine, he made a U-turn and spun out, spreading sand behind him in all directions.

Good, that'll send the message that the days of trespassin' is over.

* * *

By the look of the retiring sun, it was close to 6:00 p.m. when the roar of the motor on the jon boat took Otis out into Blackwater Bay. The wind no longer whipped the waves into a frenzy and a calmness settled over the water. Otis breathed heartily of the fresh air and took his time meandering along Robinson Point. Not much along the coast had changed, and that brought a sense of relief. He recognized several reliable floundering grounds in the shallows and decided to sit and wait for darkness to wipe out lingering rays of light. He looked up into the sky and noted that no moon was visible. *That's good*, he told himself. *Flounder tend to be skittish in the moonlight. Better to be dark so I can see their red eyes and mesmerize them with the light. Just hope I haven't lost my touch. Not much floundering done in prison.*

After a few minutes, Otis picked up the spear and began to gig. Several rusty attempts to spear the fish failed, but he finally nailed one. With each aim, Otis improved his skill and the cooler no longer was empty. Without warning, as the sixth flounder wiggled and slithered against the sides of the barrier, a shot shattered the early evening stillness.

Somebody coon huntin' I reckon. Seems a little early. Coons roam around in the dead of night.

Another shot. Otis listened, and the sound of a barking dog followed the shots. He chuckled to himself. *Bet that dog got him a coon cornered up a tree. You ain't got a chance, coon. Oh, well, I'm out here to flounder, not to worry 'bout some night-stalkin animal. I know what's gonna be on my supper table tonight.*

For the next fifteen minutes, a continual yowl drifted through the darkening night. Its mournful resonance struck a nerve within Otis and he lost interest in floundering. *Somethin' ain't right over yonder. That dog's whinning is sendin' chills up my spine. Time to check this out.*

Chapter Three

"Don't answer it, sweetie," begged the strawberry blond sitting across the table from her date. "This is the first evening in a month we've had together." A strand of red hair fell across her pouting face.

"Have too, honey. I'm on call. You know my partner took the week off. Conner's a new daddy now, and I wouldn't deny him the time he needs to help Heather and the baby get settled into a new routine." Nick Melino reached into the left pocket of his jacket and produced his cell phone.

"Melino, here. What's up, Andy?"

Sheriff Kendall told me to call you, Lieutenant. There's been a shooting out on Blackwater Bay."

"Another drug runner get his?"quipped Nick.

"Not this time, Nick."

The sober tone in the dispatcher's voice disturbed Nick. "What happened, Andy?"

"You sitting down, sir?"

"Yes, as a matter of fact I'm about to order dinner, but I don't like the sound of this, buddy." Nick looked over at his date, Maureen, whose demeanor changed to concern.

Andy relayed the news. "We got a call from an employee at the marina down on Blackwater Bay who told us a guy pulled up about eight o'clock shouting at them to call the sheriff's office. He said there was a party barge out on the Blackwater adrift with a barking dog and a dead man slumped over the steering wheel."

Nick shook his head to the left and right and signaled to the approaching waiter to back off while he listened to every detail.

"So, where is he now?"

"That's the strange part—according to the caller he took off. Didn't even get out of his boat."

'Somethin' amiss there, Andy. I'll be paying them a visit."

"Yes, sir. The patrol guys just towed the barge into the landing at Peterson Point and they're waiting for you."

Nick placed his napkin on the table and pushed back his chair. "I'm on my way. Has forensics been called? Tell them their boss is with me. She'll need her work clothes and tool box. Talk to you la—"

Before Nick could finish, Andy cut in. "Nick, it was Judge Ramsey."

The color drained from Nick's face and his response was disbelief. "What? Are they sure?"

"Everyone knows Judge Ramsey, Nick. There's no doubt."

Maureen saw the shock on her date's face, rushed to his side, and grabbed onto his arm to steady his six-foot frame.

"C'mon, you need some cool air. We're out of here."

Once outside, Nick sketched out the conversation and took a deep breath of air to regain his control before he continued in a cracking voice, "The judge and I go back a long ways. I saved his daughter's life when her car crashed and she was pinned behind the wheel. He was so grateful. He never turned me down when I needed his legal help with court orders and such." Rising anger replaced any weakness in his voice. "I'll hunt the scum down 'til the day I die."

In twenty minutes, Nick's Camaro came to an abrupt stop at the bay's edge. Portable lights surrounded the barge and surveillance tape kept any curiosity seekers away from the scene. Within seconds, the forensics van pulled up beside Nick's car.

Maureen was on the job as quick as she could ditch the heels, grab her crocs, and zip up her jumpsuit.

Anxious to ID the body himself, Nick ducked under the tape and boarded the barge. Lying on the deck near the bow was a man who, in Nick's mind, was the epitome of what a man should be. Tears blinded his eyes as they surveyed the judge's wounded, bloody body.

Maureen took one glance at Nick and took charge.

"Fellas, bring that high-powered lantern closer to the body. Anthony, you start collecting blood samples. Check the railings, steering wheel, etcetera, for prints, too."

Whimpering, with a downcast expression, a golden lab had one paw lying across the judge's shoulder while his face nuzzled his master's neck.

Maureen bent over the body and began her inspection. Hindered by the dog's presence, she asked Nick, "Could you try and move him? I need to get in there." Her voice was tender and she reached out and put a soothing hand on the animal's head. "I know, feller, it's hard to lose someone you love."

A mournful groan erupted from the animal's throat as Nick grasped his collar and gently dragged him away from the body. A trail of blood, blocked by the pressure of the dog, trickled down from a gaping hole on the left side of the judge's neck.

Upon further investigation, Maureen located a second wound close to the heart.

"The poor man never had a chance," she sighed. "Let's get him to the morgue, boys. I'll do a thorough examination in the morning."

With the body bag secured in the back of the van, Maureen slammed the doors, walked over to Nick, and pressed her cheek to his. "I'm so sorry you've lost a dear friend. Tomorrow we'll both hit the ground running. Whoever did this doesn't have a chance—not with my guy after him."

Nick squeezed her arm and whispered, "Your support means everything to me. Right now, I need to break the news to Mrs. Ramsey. It won't be easy. Goodnight, hon. Talk to you in the morning."

Nick walked back to the waiting officers and looked at the dog. "Well, ole fella, I guess I need to take you home to your mistress." Nick's voice trembled, "I'm not the man she's expectin' in from floundering. I can assure you of that."

"Lieutenant, don't worry. We're here for the night. No one's going to disturb the scene."

Nick thanked his officers and turned to go when he had a second thought. "Guys, I'm not going to take the dog all covered in the judge's blood. Mrs. Ramsey doesn't need to see that. Mind if he stays here a while longer? Oh, and did you see anyone near the barge when you got there?"

Both men shook their heads back and forth indicating a negative response.

"Hmm, strange. You'd think the guy would've stuck around. Most folks can't wait to hear all the gory details. I'll have to think on that awhile. See you in the morning."

Chapter Four

The moment Nick turned the ignition key of his car, a flood of nauseous grief churned in the pit of his stomach and threatened to send him retching into the bushes. For the better part of twenty-five years, the sight of a dead body became routine and he learned to keep his emotions in tow. Only twice in his career did he fail. Five years ago, a close high school friend was found dead behind a sand dune after attending a reunion. Now, the death of a dear friend struck again. The sight of Judge Henry Ramsey's shattered body shook his staunch composure.

Nick took several deep breaths and the fluttering in his stomach calmed down. He knew a long night lay ahead of him, but he had a job to do. Glenda Ramsey must hear the grim news that her husband was dead. *And I must be the one to tell her.* As Nick gathered his thoughts, he remembered the judge telling him that his wife's health was a major reason he intended to retire in six months.

"She suffered a heart attack," explained Judge Ramsey. "Not a major one, but serious enough to scare both of us. She spent a week in the hospital and I brought her home last evening. I made up my mind then and there that I've sat behind this bench long enough. Bless her heart, after all these years she deserves to come first in my life. I sent in my resignation effective in six months."

This news could finish her, thought Nick. *She can't be alone. Sarah needs to be with her mother.* Not having the judge's daughter's number listed on his cell, Nick rummaged under the passenger's seat and pulled out a tattered phone directory. *Married name…married name?* An old trick he learned in middle school came back to him. *When in doubt, start with the alphabet. a…b…c Cooper, that's it. Sarah Cooper. Husband's name, Daniel.*

Nick's eyes bore into the page until he found the number. In seconds, his fingers punched the cell's keyboard and he waited for someone to answer.

A man's voice responded, and Nick's professional demeanor relayed the shattering news. The conversation was short. Nick didn't want to waste time going into detail. Besides, he had nothing to go on at this point. He closed by making a request. "Please meet me at the judge's home. I think it best, considering Mrs. Ramsey's condition, that she have family with her when I tell her what's happened. I'm on my way."

In ten minutes, Nick reached his destination. A Chevy Malibu tailed him up the lane and pulled up beside his Camaro. Out of habit, Nick checked the inside pocket of his jacket for his pen and notebook before he got out. It was the one article he favored over any electronic recording device. Simple but trustworthy. Experience taught him to be prepared to record the smallest detail.

Sarah rushed to his side, her pixie face ashen and distraught. "Lieutenant, all my life I've lived in dread of this day. Late night threatening calls and anonymous notes in our mailbox were no strangers to my father. He dismissed them as pure hoaxes. This time, he was wrong."

Nick looked into her watering eyes and swallowed a lump in his throat before answering. "I'm so sorry, Sarah."

He gathered her crumpling body in his arms and held her while a floodgate of tears soaked into the lapel of his jacket. After several moments, her husband took over and said, "C'mon, baby, we've got to tell your mama."

At that moment, a front door opened and a woman in her seventies dressed in a robe adjusted her wire-rimmed glasses and called, "Sarah, is that you and Daniel?" The porch light helped confirm her curiosity, but it took a moment before she recognized Nick. "And Lieutenant Melino?"

"Yes, ma'am."

"I'm sorry, but Henry isn't home. You know how he loves to fish. It's regular routine for him after dinner to take the dog on the barge and go out on the bay. I think it clears his mind after making decisions in court all day."

Glenda stopped talking for a second and looked at her wrist watch before continuing, "It's getting late, though. He normally is home by now." She turned her attention to her son-in-law. "You don't suppose he had motor trouble, do you, Daniel? It was overhauled last week."

Finally, Sarah spoke up. "Mama, we have to talk to you."

Glenda's hands flew up to her porcelain-smooth face. "Pardon my manners. Yes, y'all come in." Once inside, she looked at her daughter and asked, "Sarah, are you feeling all right? Your cheeks are flushed, dear."

Sarah took her mother's hand and led her to the sofa, where she started to explain the horrifying circumstances. "Mama, Daddy isn't coming home tonight." She tried to continue, but the words refused to form. She turned her head toward Nick, pleading with her eyes. The silent message was clear, and he finished the task he knew he had to do.

As Nick expected, Glenda fell apart and her sobs came from the depths of her soul. Sarah rocked her shaking mother in her arms. Every few seconds, she wiped the unending flow of tears from reddened eyes. Finally, a sense of calm settled over her frail body.

Nick stood up to leave, but before he did, he took hold of Glenda's hands and looked into a broken-hearted face. "Mrs. Ramsey, your husband taught me so much about what it means to be a decent human being without ever lecturing from a book. His life *was* the book, and he lived each page to the best of his ability. I promise you, my department will find out who did this."

Both Daniel and Sarah nodded their heads in agreement while Glenda, her voice almost a whisper, replied, "I know you will, Lieutenant. Henry bragged on you every time he had a case that you were involved in."

"Thank you, ma'am. You know, I will have to talk to you during this investigation. There are many questions. But not tonight. I'll come by when you feel like talking. Meantime, if there's anything I can do, don't hesitate to ask. Goodnight."

Daniel walked Nick to the door, shook his hand, and asked in a lowered voice, "Will she have to identify the body?"

"Only if she wants to. It's not a pretty scene. Forensics will take prints and they'll match those on record. Keep me posted on all the funeral arrangements. I know the officers will want to show their respects with a cavalcade."

"Will do, Lieutenant. Thanks for taking your time to make it personal."

Nick patted Daniel's shoulder as he opened the door. "That's the easy part. Tomorrow's when the work begins. Oh, I almost forgot. The dog's still with the officers. He's covered in the judge's blood, and I didn't want Glenda to see that."

Daniel shook his head in agreement. "I appreciate your concern, Lieutenant. I'll take care of it. Good night."

Chapter Five

Panic sent Otis's heart racing. His breathing accelerated and he gasped for breath the moment his light fell on the face of the man whose countenance was ingrained in his memory for eighteen years.

Otis's first thought was to head back to his camp immediately, but deep within his conscience another voice struggled to be heard. *You can't leave a dead man and his dog adrift. T'ain't human—ain't right.* Otis grappled with the situation. On one hand he justified it was well-deserved revenge—but on the other, could he live knowing he'd abandoned a fellow human being?

With one hand on the barge's railing, Otis took a couple of deep breaths to calm his jangled nerves and made his decision. One quick tug on his boat's rope released it from the tie-down cleat and he jumped over the bow to maneuver his way back to the Evinrude motor. Within seconds, he felt the breeze in his face as he steered his craft toward the marina a mile down the bay.

Lights surrounded the docking area and flickered like neon on the rippled water. Two men carried an outboard motor down a ramp and started to enter the main building.

Stay in the shadows—not to close to the lights, cautioned Otis's inner voice. *They's not so likely to recognize a black man.*

Instantly, Otis cut the throttle on the motor and took a deep breath to expand his lungs, then shouted, "Hey, man! Call the sheriff's office. There's a dead man adrift on a party boat 'bout a mile down yonder."

His words caught the men by surprise. They staggered under their heavy load and turned toward the water.

"What'd you say?" asked the owner of the marina. "A dead man?"

Before they had time to come closer, Otis pressed the start button on the motor's ignition and sped off into the darkness. His shaking hands found it difficult to hold the boat on a steady course and the wake behind him formed a zigzag pattern. Finally, instinct directed Otis to his camp and the bow of his boat gave him a jolt as it bumped against the side of the dock. He looked around to see if anyone was in sight and emptied the vessel of fishing gear, lantern and cooler. Within record time, everything was stowed in its proper place. Only one job remained. The flounder needed filleting if he was to have fish to eat.

He picked up the fillet knife, ran his thumb across the blade to check for sharpness, and placed it under a gill to make the first cut. Blood oozed out from the incision and a chill, accompanied by the memory of the dead man's blood, paralyzed his hand.

Run, man, run! A voice echoed in his ears. *They's gonna git you!* Otis shook his head and tried to shake away the words, but it persisted, *You the first man they'll suspect. Fresh outa prison and people knows you hated the man for your sentence. You best hit the road.*

Otis refused to comply and forced his knife to complete the task at hand. Blood and guts spilled out of the flounder's stomach, leaving an empty cavity. One swift move of his hand and off came the flounder's head. Instantly, another head flashed before him—a human head covered in blood.

A drink. I need a drink, thought Otis. *Something to take away the memory. Gotta be some booze around here somewhere.* No sooner had he entertained this thought when his mama's words stopped him cold. *Lawdy, ain't nothin' good ever come of the devil's drink. Won't git ya nuthin' but a heap of trouble.*

Otis let the memory of her words sink in and he conceded she was right. After eighteen years in prison, his desire for alcohol dried up after he saw what it had done to many of his fellow prisoners. Some of them suffered torturing tremors along with other withdrawal symptoms. Gaunt, sunken eyes pleaded for one more swig from a bottle and pale, expressionless faces stared into space.

Every time he encountered one of these men, his mama's warning rang true. However, in his younger years it was a different story for Owen and him. Her words often fell on deaf ears and both boys suffered minor consequences. Now, with a clearer vision, Otis knew alcohol wouldn't erase what he saw on the party barge this evening, nor would it calm his jangled nerves.

With the last fish filleted, he put down the knife, sat on the edge of the dock, and let the sounds of the night surround him. A lonely bullfrog croaked and in seconds out of the bulrushes rose a chorus of females answering his call. Water lapped against the dock timbers and he could feel its rhythm. It had a mesmerizing effect on Otis, and out of nowhere a strange feeling stirred in the recesses of his mind. It inched forward until the words of an old hymn took center stage. *Where could I go but to the Lord?*

An unexplainable relief washed truth over his trembling body and he made a decision. Running away would cast suspicion on him. The song grew louder and he visualized a church choir swaying and singing in perfect harmony to the rhythm of the melody. It sent him to his knees.

I's got nowhere to hide, Lord. You know I didn't pull no trigger to kill the judge, but they's gonna figure I got the motive. Sure 'nuff.

By now, tears washed Otis's cheeks clean. *Please, Lawd, don't let them send me back to no prison.*

Between sobs, he continued his plea until exhaustion won the upper hand and he stumbled into his camp cabin and sleep obliterated the day's events.

Chapter Six

Nick tossed and turned all night. The sheets, twisted and tangled, looked as though they'd been in the midst of a tornado. The image of Judge Ramsey's limp body draped over the boat's steering wheel with his loyal dog, Callie, snuggled close to his master took precedence over a wink of sleep.

It isn't fair. He didn't deserve to die this way. How many men and women owed him a debt of gratitude for changing the course of their lives from a life of crime to one of rehabilitation?

Nick reached over to his bedside table and turned off the alarm clock. It wasn't needed this morning. Reluctantly, he raised his tired body and sat on the edge of the bed. He ran a hand down the side of his whisker-stubbled face while a dull throbbing at the base of his skull worked its way up the sides of his head and settled in his temples.

Coffee. I want coffee, he mused. *Caffeine's the only antidote I need to nip this headache in the bud. Gotta think clearly today. A cold shower wouldn't hurt either.* The thought of the latter sent a chill throughout his fatigued six-foot frame, but he bucked up and let the pulsating water revive his senses. He was anxious to get the forensics' initial report, but he knew Maureen and her team would not rush their examination.

As Nick slid a towel across his chest to capture lingering beads of water, he caught sight of himself in the full-length mirror. He winced at his once-taut stomach that now bore signs of a midlife paunch. Guilt assaulted him—too many fast food dinner stops now resulted in a broadening waistline.

Nick imagined his daughter's scolding the next time she came home.

Dad, eating out every night will kill you. You're not eating the proper food, are you? I knew this would happen as soon as I moved to the Keys.

Nick smiled. *I love you, Penny, but there are times your nagging sounds just like your mom. Not a great quality, honey. It can lead to divorce.*

Not wishing to linger on the negative aspects of marriage, his thoughts returned to Maureen. A warm, tingling sensation enveloped his body from head to toe every time he reflected on her fit body and thick reddish-blonde hair that framed a heart-shaped face. A sprinkling of freckles across the bridge of her nose added to her allure.

Nick couldn't deny that for the past year, she'd brought a dimension of joy to his life. *Of course the fact that she turns every male head in the sheriff's office and has chosen to spend time with me is pure bliss.*

One last peek in the mirror as he slapped aftershave on his cheeks exposed another truth. *Man, you need a haircut. Where'd all this gray come from anyway?*

Nick suspected all this introspection was his defense mechanism working to help him stop dwelling on the judge's death. By the time he got to work, he knew the investigation would be the only subject on his mind.

Like a man on a mission, Nick entered the building and headed straight for the lounge. The smell of coffee grounds percolating his favorite fragrance was a good thing. It took three cups to calm the aching beast in his head. As he swallowed the last mouthful, Conner, appeared at the doorway.

Surprised to see him, Nick asked. "What are you doing here? I thought you intended to take a week off and help your lovely wife with your new son. Everything going okay?"

Conner, red-eyed and weary, shuffled toward the coffee maker. "You didn't tell me I'd be up half the night walking the floor trying to sooth a crying baby. What's this colic, anyway?"

Nick shrugged his shoulders. "Beats me. I'm a detective, not a doctor. Don't think Penny ever had it—least if she did, her mother took care of it. Don't worry, pal, this too shall pass. At Colin's college graduation, you'll never think of all the sleep you lost." Nick gave Conner a friendly slap on his shoulder.

Conner frowned at Nick and let out a sigh of indignation. "Thanks. You're such a help. Heather told me to go back to work. If she needs help, she'll call her grandmother who has practically moved in anyway."

Nick changed the subject and his face grew serious. "I suppose you heard the morning news about Judge Ramsey?"

Conner nodded in the affirmative before answering. "On the radio as I pulled into the parking lot. Did Kendall put us on the case?"

"Yes. Even if he hadn't, I would have asked for it. I think you know how I respected that man." Nick wiped his eyes before tears blurred his vision. "It was a grim scene last night. Shot in the head and one more went through his heart according, to Maureen."

"Sounds as though someone meant to finish him off. I understand from the radio report that he was out on the Blackwater on his party barge. Whoever did it had to know he'd be out there, don't ya think?"

"Oh, yeah, you're right. Henry's routine must have been watched for awhile. Many a time he told me fishing on the Blackwater was his release from all the crap he had to deal with every day. It's going to be the proverbial needle in a haystack identifying suspects with the number of resentful folks who were not happy with his final judgments."

Before Conner commented, Sheriff Kendall walked by the lounge, caught sight of his two detectives, wheeled around, and entered the room.

"Morning, fellas. Melino, thank you for personally taking the news to Mrs. Ramsey last night. Her son-in-law called me this morning to say the family appreciated the way it was handled. It's a sad day for Santa Rosa County. Judge Ramsey was a man of integrity and these days that's a quality our society is sorely lacking."

"No doubt about that," replied Conner.

Nick entered the conversation. "We'll find his killer, Sheriff. We owe it to him for the many times he gave us a wide berth when we needed his legal help."

Sheriff Kendall reached for a cup and poured the last of the coffee before he spoke. "I assured the State Attorney that I've put the best two men I have on this case so I want you to use every resource we have to solve it." Kendall started to say more, hesitated, then continued, "I'm not sure how to put this because I hate it when politics get involved in our work. But because of the judge's reputation throughout the state of Florida, I'm afraid we're going to be put under a microscope. In other words, this investigation will go right up to the governor. Get my point?"

"I hear you—top priority."

Sheriff Kendall gave Nick and Conner a thumbs up and was almost out the door when he remembered something.

"Oh, Nick, do you remember an early case you worked on involving a carjacking and the death of a sleeping child in the back seat? Almost twenty years ago."

Nick pursed his lips as he searched his memory. Within seconds he started to spout details. "Yes, I do. A black man went to prison for that one. I recall it shocked me at the time because he owned a fish camp down on the Blackwater. Seemed like a decent sort. Dad and I always put our boat in there and he had the best bait on the river. Why do you ask?"

Kendall explained, "I got a call from the warden over at the prison. This man was released two days ago. Served eighteen years. Before you start work on Judge Ramsey's investigation, I think it'd be a good idea to give the victim a call and let her know Otis Washington's a free man. I'm not expecting any trouble from him, but you never know what he might be thinking after all this time. I'll have one of the girls pull his file and bring it over to you."

"Otis Washington. Hmm…" muttered Nick as he rinsed out his cup and put it back in the cupboard.

Conner recognized the signs as he looked at his boss. "Okay, I see the wheels are turning. What's the deal with this man?"

"I think we just got our first lead, partner. Judge Ramsey sentenced Washington to twenty years in prison!"

Chapter Seven

Samuel Wilson adjusted a silk tie around the collar of his French cuff shirt as he prepared for another day in court. The sports announcer on the TV caught his attention at the mention of March Madness–college basketball at its finest. A grimace crossed his flawless tanned face when he heard the discouraging news. The University of Kentucky 40—Florida Gators 26.

No way, he exclaimed. *What a way to start my day! When are those guys going to pull it together? Sure not like it used to be in my day.* He glanced over his shoulder at a glass display case. Inside, championship memorabilia consisted of signed basketballs, a number 12 jersey, team photos that celebrated victory, and numerous newspaper clippings. One headline stood out among the others: "Slamin' Sam" does it again!

Sam reflected on that heady feeling. Making slam dunks in front of thousands of screaming college kids was the best high in the world to him. *Yeah*, he mused, *we were good. Seems as though* this *year's team is afraid to take risks. Playing it too safe and lettin' the competition steam roll 'em. They've got to take control of the ball and keep it. Just like dad used to say, "Sam, if you want to succeed, you have to take control."*

Sam slipped on his tailor-made suit jacket and started to straighten out the blankets on his side of the bed. For a moment, he stopped and stared at the empty undisturbed spot next to him. It was once claimed by his wife. Claudette's biting words continued to ring in his ears. "I can't stay married to a control freak any longer. Nothing I do is right. You're so consumed with making a name for yourself in the law community, you've forgotten I'm supposed to be your partner. There's more to life than seeing to it that every Tom, Dick, and Harry that comes to court ends up behind bars. I feel as though I'm one of your prisoners."

Gone for six months now, Sam accepted the fact that Claudette was not coming back. *Fine, have it your way, baby. There's plenty of others waiting to fill that empty spot.* A smirk tickled the edges of Sam's lips and the cleft in his chiseled chin broadened as once more college memories flooded back to him. *Being a "big man on campus" certainly had its rewards.* Even after twenty years, Sam knew his infectious smile wooed the ladies and he had his pick of the harem.

He took one last look in the full-length mirror, pushed a strand of wheat-colored hair back in its proper place, and strutted down the stairs. He was halfway out the front door when the familiar jiggle on his cell phone hidden inside his jacket brought him to an abrupt stop.

Before answering, he looked at the I.D. information. No surprise there. He proceeded to answer.

"Yeah. What's up?"

"You hear the news this mornin'?" asked a male caller.

"Disgusting isn't it? My Gators let me down again."

"I ain't talkin' 'bout no Gators. Judge Ramsey's been found dead."

"What? You sure?" Sam continued to question. Heart attack? Stroke? What killed him?"

"Shot to death on his party barge."

"No way! I have a case scheduled before him today."

"Ain't gonna happen. And why didn't you answer your cell last night? We was supposed to meet."

Sam continued to needle. "Heavy date last night. Didn't want any interruptions."

"So some gal more important than our business?"

Annoyance crept into Sam's voice. "Look, Washington, you owed me one. I kept your sorry hide out of prison for eighteen years and don't you forget it."

Washington came right back. "And I've been your supplier all these years. Never once mentioned your name. You got everybody in this here town lookin' up to the high and mighty State Attorney" A sneering laugh caught Sam by surprise. "What I know about you would blow the lid off your big ambitions."

Sam took a deep breath and got hold of his emotions. *Won't do to get him all riled up. He knows he's holding the right cards. I need to placate him with more cash. Always works.*

"Calm down, man, I'll sweeten the pot. Meet me at the fish camp just after dark. Say 8:30 tonight."

'Not no more. My brother's done his time and 'cordin to my kin he's moved back in. Gonna have to find us a new spot."

"That's your job, Owen. That is if you don't want your cash supply drying up."

Another taunting laugh wrangled Sam's nerves. "Not likely to happen. In fact, you and I got lots in common. Now that makes us almost like brothers wouldn't you say? 'Cept for our tans—mine's a little darker than yours." Another laugh ended the conversation. "Later, dude."

Chapter Eight

The ringing of Tracy Sloan's phone interrupted her first chore of the morning. She pulled her soapy hands out of the dishwater, grabbed a towel, and reached for the receiver.

"Hello."

"Tracy Sloan?" asked Nick.

"Yes," replied the woman expecting some high-powered sales pitch. "But I'm very busy and I don't have time to talk."

Quick to identify himself, Nick began, "This is Lieutenant Nick Melino of the Sheriff's Office. I need to talk to you, ma'am. It's important, but I promise I won't take up too much time."

A sigh of relief traveled through the line before Tracy spoke. "I apologize, Lieutenant, but these days it seems every other caller is someone trying to lure me into some deal or another. I find myself constantly on the defensive. Now what is it you wanted to tell me?"

"We got a call from the prison warden this week. Otis Washington is out of prison after serving eighteen years."

Tracy gasped. Without hesitation, memories of that unbearable night flooded her mind and her trembling voice whimpered, "I'm sorry. I wasn't expecting that news."

"We aren't anticipating any problems from him, but you do have the right to know he's in the area."

"Thank you, Lieutenant. I promise I'll be vigilant, but the timing of your call is interesting."

"Why's that, ma'am?"

"Well, about ten days ago I was feeling depressed. It was my baby's eighteenth birthday." Nick sensed the woman fighting for control. "MaryJane would have graduated from high school this coming June." A sniffle interrupted her story.

"Throughout the years, when I feel the need to connect to my child, I go to the cedar chest where I've stored her clothes, toys, photos. You know, memorabilia. I realize it may sound weird to you, but it gives me comfort to touch them."

"Not at all, Mrs. Sloan. Each of us has our own way to deal with personal loss."

"At the bottom of the chest I'd forgotten I'd put the sweater I wore that dreadful night. Why did I save it? I'm not sure, but I can tell you I felt compelled to pull it out of the chest."

Nick began to wonder where this woman was going with her narrative and his patience grew thinner. He was at the point where he didn't have time to listen to meandering when she astounded him with her next statement.

"Otis Washington was not the man who dragged me out of the car."

"Excuse me? Did I hear correctly? You're saying Otis Washington is innocent? How can that be? You identified him."

"Lieutenant, I've had ten years of psychiatric therapy to try and come to terms with my daughter's death. I've blamed myself over and over. The questions keep returning. Why did I stop at that particular convenience store? I was one mile from home. I could have filled my gas tank the next day. It wasn't even empty. Did I not scream loud enough for the attendants inside to hear me? Nothing the psychiatrist said to me gave me peace. As a last resort, the doctor put me under hypnosis. He thought if I relived the events I would finally realize it wasn't my fault and that I did everything a mother could do under the circumstances."

Nick picked up a pen and started to write on his notepad as he listened to Tracy unravel her story.

"It was at our last session I saw it again."

Nick straightened in his chair. Tracy Sloan captured Nick's full attention. "What was it you saw?"

"A Medic Alert symbol. The sweater has a tear the size of a quarter in the left arm up near the shoulder. That's where a link on the gold bracelet the man was wearing caught in the yarn. He struggled with it and of course I could see the threads embedded between the links. Finally, in anger, he yanked it free and tossed me out of the car."

"Okay, but how does that prove Otis is innocent? I'm not following you."

"I gave the prosecutor a description of the bracelet that attached itself to my sweater. But the bracelet I was told to identify in court had no symbol, nor were there any threads of yarn attached to it."

It took Nick a few seconds to digest the implication of what this woman confessed.

"So you're telling me after all these years, you believe the bracelet you identified in court was not the one snagged to your sweater."

"Yes, Lieutenant. That's what I'm telling you. When the prosecutor asked me to identify the bracelet, all I saw was a plain, gold-linked one. I assumed he had the correct one. Please understand the duress I was under. At that point, all gold bracelets would have looked the same to me. Details of any particular one were irrelevant."

"The bracelet was one piece of evidence the jury used to convict Otis." Nick continued, "Are you sure it wasn't the same bracelet that caught in your sweater?"

"Yes, I'm sure. My husband is allergic to penicillin and he wears a Medic Alert symbol on his watch."

"Mrs. Sloan, what you are suggesting is a very serious matter and it could mean opening up the case again."

"I know that, Lieutenant. That's why I took the sweater and my story over a week ago to State Attorney Wilson and Robert Swift. Do you know him? He was Mr. Washington's defense attorney." Tracy sobbed, "And now the poor judge who heard the case is dead."

Nick ran his hand through his hair and took a deep breath. What he intended as a courtesy call turned his morning upside down. No longer did he have a murder to solve but now a new facet in an old case could not be ignored—someone other than Otis Washington may have gotten away with murder.

Chapter Nine

Nick put his head in his hands and tried to collect his thoughts. For the time being, he needed to concentrate on Judge Ramsey's death, not on a crime that happened years ago. He was in this frame of mind when Conner walked into the office and asked, "Hey partner, you okay? You look a little distraught."

Nick raised his head and said, "Just when we think a case is cut and dry, justice served, time to file it under solved, out of left field comes possible new evidence that could clear a man's name."

Conner pulled up a chair. A questioning expression on his face urged Nick to continue his dialogue.

"Did you hear the sheriff tell me when we were in the lounge this morning that a man by the name of Otis Washington is out of prison?"

Conner nodded. "Told you to call the victim. Let her know."

"I talked to her fifteen minutes ago, and now she claims she is positive the wrong man went to prison."

Conner's face went white. "Tell me it isn't so. The one fear I've had in this job is that we'd arrest the wrong person. Maybe she's wrong."

"One way or the other, it can't be ignored. She's already taken her story to both the State Attorney and Washington's defense attorney. That means the sentencing judge who happened to be Judge Ramsey would normally call a meeting of the two."

"Too late for that," Conner commented.

"It might have already happened. I'll get in touch with the defense attorney and ask him. Meantime, we have to get busy on the judge's murder." Nick opened a file folder marked Ramsey and started making notes. "First on our agenda is access into the judge's chamber. Call down to the court house and see who will give us a search warrant. I'll check things out with forensics. I'm hoping they've done their examination. We need some concrete facts."

"I'm on it, partner. No doubt they're expecting us at the court house this morning, so a search warrant shouldn't be a problem."

"Just want to cover our bases," returned Nick.

The sound of Nick's fingers drumming the top of his desk escalated in intensity while he waited for someone to answer at forensics. Finally, a voice Nick recognized responded. "Forensics, may I help you?"

"Andy, Melino here. Is Maureen able to talk right now?"

"We just finished a child's autopsy and we're cleaning up, but I'll tell her to pick up the phone."

Nick heard the running of water from the hoses used to wash down the examining table, utensils, and floor. Blood and other bodily excretions from a corpse left a putrid smell after an autopsy. The vision was thoroughly embedded in his memory. He'd witnessed the procedure more times than he cared to count. One thing he knew for sure—Maureen's eagle eye would see to it that the room met all cleanliness standards.

A tender voice he'd come to value broke the reverie. "Morning, Nick. How'd you sleep last night? Awful I bet."

"I kept seeing the judge over and over. It wasn't a good night. This whole morning's been a bummer so far. Hope you've got something we can go on. Kendall tells me the pressure's on from Tallahassee to move fast."

"I realize," Maureen reminded him "that this is a top priority case so that makes it all the more important we don't miss anything. The autopsy is scheduled for one o'clock this afternoon."

Before Maureen could elaborate, Nick cut in. "You mean you haven't started yet?" Impatience and lack of sleep gave a critical edge to his voice.

"And I don't want you here when we do," Maureen answered with authority. "You're too upset and close to the victim. I want to concentrate on my job. The last thing I need is to have you fall apart physically and emotionally when I make the first cut"

Nick knew she was correct. He wouldn't handle it well. He admired Judge Ramsey too much.

"I'm sorry, hon. Forgive me. Just promise me one thing,"

"What's that?"

Nick's persuasive voice returned, "Have dinner with me tonight. I owe it to you since you didn't get a chance to even order last evening. Please."

A moment of hesitation on Maureen's part gave the appearance of doubt and Nick held his breath. *I shouldn't have snapped at her,* her reasoned. *Serves me right.*

Relief washed over him when he heard her response.

"Sounds fine. I have a feeling that after I finish what's before me today, I won't feel like taking the effort to cook for myself. Same place? Same time?"

"Yes. David's Catfish House it is."

* * *

The mood at the courthouse was somber. From the security guards at the front entrance to the custodian sweeping the floor, sadness prevailed.

There was no need for anyone to direct Nick and Conner to Judge Ramsey's chamber. They'd traveled that route many times in the past when a warrant from the judge was issued. It was never denied.

On the glass paneled door that led into the secretary's outer office, a piece of paper notified the public that the Honorable Samuel Ramsey had died. Funeral arrangements were pending.

Mary Murphy, a middle-aged office manager, looked up from her computer at the sound of the opening door. Swollen, red eyes met the detectives and her sadness could not be contained.

"Lieutenant, isn't it awful? To think someone took his life. And with only four more months until he planned to retire. I almost stayed home today, I'm so sick about it."

Mary pulled a tissue from a box beside her keyboard and dabbed at her nose. "But I decided it's best to be here to answer the phone. The calls are already starting to pour in."

Mary looked at Nick with questioning eyes before she asked, "He'd want me to do that, don't you think?" Another tear rolled down her blush-smeared cheek.

Nick walked toward her and did his best to console this lady who'd spent the last fifteen years as a faithful friend and employee to Judge Ramsey. "You're exactly where you need to be, Mary." He patted her shoulder and continued, "Your dedication speaks volumes of how you respected him. He'd be proud."

"Thank you, Lieutenant. It's the least I can do for him now."

Conner cleared his throat and asked, "Can you unlock his chamber, ma'am? We need to look around and see if anything is amiss. Do you know if the judge was the last person to leave his office yesterday?"

"Well, let me see." Mary flipped open her calendar notebook. "I left at five and no one was scheduled to have an appointment with him after that. Of course now and again some of his peers drop by just to chat. Mostly something about the law or men talk—fishing, golf, you know what I mean."

Mary's cheeks flushed pink and she quickly explained herself. "Sounds as though I was eavesdropping, but as you can see there's a small hallway from this office to his and sometimes the door was left open."

The detectives gave her a reassuring smile and Nick repeated Conner's request to open the chamber.

"Yes, yes, gentlemen come on back."

The moment Nick walked into Judge Ramsey's chambers he felt the man's presence. A large framed copy of the United States Constitution hung on the wall directly behind a mahogany desk. Rows of law books filled two book cases, and attached to one end wall hung the Stars and Stripes along with Florida's flag. Interspersed throughout the room the warmth Henry Ramsey felt for his family appeared evident in the collection of photos.

For a few seconds, neither detective spoke. The lump in Nick's throat prevented him from speaking and disturbing the reverence this room demanded.

Finally Conner broke the silence. "Everything looks orderly and the way I expect he left it every day. On the surface I don't see any sign of a break-in. Do you?"

"I doubt we will, but I couldn't leave this stone unturned. Clues have a way of showing up in the darndest places. The killer knew he wouldn't have a chance here with all the security. That's why he picked some obscure location. Better chance of getting away."

Nick walked over to the desk and noticed a familiar file folder used by court reporters. The words on the title caught his eye and he read them aloud. "The State of Florida VS Otis Washington."

Conner's ears perked up and he asked, "What did you say?"

"Come here," Nick instructed. "Look at this. It's the trial transcript of that black fella I told you about. So this must mean the judge intended to have a meeting with the State Attorney and Washington's lawyer."

"Wonder when?" Conner asked then turned toward the door. "Mary would know. Let me go get her."

"Good idea. Ask her to join us."

The click of a woman's heels on the tile floor kept up with the long stride of the detective's legs.

Nick picked up the transcript and asked. "How long has this been on the desk?"

Mary came closer to examine the title. "About ten days, I believe." Her brows knit together as she thought about the question. "Yes, I remember now. I had a dentist appointment that afternoon and was on my way out of the office when the judge asked me to run over to archives and bring him this transcript. I hurried because I didn't want to be late for my appointment. It took a little searching. After all, the trial was eighteen years ago, but I found it."

"Do you know why he wanted it?" Conner's curiosity grew.

"All I know is that when I handed it to him, he thanked me and instructed me to call Robert Swift and Samuel Wilson to set up a mutual appointment."

"Did that meeting take place this week?" inquired Nick.

"Three days ago. It's not unusual for the State Attorney and a defense attorney to meet, but I got the impression it didn't turn out well."

Conner pulled out a chair and offered it to Mary. At the same time, Nick reached into his jacket pocket, extracted his notepad and pen, then said, "Might as well be comfortable, Mary. I've got several questions you may be able to shed light on."

"I'll do anything to help," she assured him.

"Why do you think there was dissension?"

"Like I told you earlier, sometimes if the door is ajar, I hear conversations. Now mind you, I'm not a gossip and what happens in this court house stays in this court house. But as the State Attorney opened the chamber door, I heard him say, "Withheld exculpatory evidence? Nonsense. I did no such thing. The man was found guilty. The bracelet was only one piece of evidence that put him behind bars."

Nick raised an eyebrow at this revelation and continued his questioning. "How did Judge Ramsey respond?"

A knowing smile crossed Mary's lips as she replied. "Gentlemen, you knew his personality. He never needed to raise his voice to get his point across. Although I heard him reply, the exact words in his calmness were not audible."

Conner chimed in, "So, in your opinion, Wilson was upset?"

"If a flushed neck and face are signs of aggravation, then Samuel Wilson was not in a good mood. In fact, the glass in my door rattled as he slammed it shut. And that's not the first time I've seen him upset."

"Oh?" both detectives spoke in unison.

"Go on," urged Nick.

"Two weeks ago, Judge Ramsey was on the phone to Mr. Wilson when I inadvertently walked into his office. He'd asked me to bring him some paperwork that needed his signature. Normally, I made all his calls so I knew this one was personal. I started to back away, but he motioned for me to come in. He told me that Samuel would be coming to see him at six o'clock that evening and to please leave a fresh pot of coffee.

"When I got home, I realized I'd left my medical bag in one of my desk drawers. Diabetes." Mary sighed as she berated herself. "Can't live without my insulin, but at times I get busy and forget, so I went back to get it about seven. Just as I opened the door, Mr. Wilson came barging through and almost knocked me down. Not even 'excuse me' or nothing. Rude if you ask me. Again, I saw the flushed face and I sensed the meeting upset him. Of course it wasn't any of my business—strictly between him and the judge."

The ringing phone in the secretary's office brought Mary to her feet. Excuse me, but I need to get that."

"No problem. Thank you for your cooperation. We won't be much longer." As Nick surveyed the desk again, his eye caught sight of a manila folder that displayed a yellow Post-It note on the cover. On it, the hand-written words "Samuel Wilson: 6:00 p.m. Tuesday, March 6" appeared to be a reminder notice.

A sliver of guilt caused Nick to pause before he flipped open the folder. *Was he crossing the line between police investigation and Judge Ramsey's personal affairs?* Mary noted that the meeting between the two men took place after business hours. In Nick's struggle to do the right thing, ethics took a back seat and he opened the folder. At the top of a page, in enlarged block letters the name Worldwide Investments stood out. As Nick scanned the document, it was obvious Judge Ramsey had entered into some financial contract. Columns of numbers which meant nothing to Nick were circled in red and the word 'explain' was written beside them.

"Hmm." Nick sighed. "Wonder what this is all about?"

Conner turned from his search and asked, "You talking to me?"

"Just thinking out loud as usual, but c'mon over and look at this."

Nick handed the folder to his partner and watched for his reaction.

After a few moments, Conner stated, "Looks like a financial statement to me. Not that I'm too familiar with investments on our salary, but apparently Judge Ramsey had business with this Worldwide outfit. Any particular reason why this strikes you as odd? The man was about to retire."

"That's not what has my attention. Look at the Post-It note. Whose name is there?

Conner flipped the cover over and said, "Samuel Wilson. You think this has something to do with him?"

"Mary told us the judge had an appointment with Mr. Wilson after hours."

"But, Nick, you and I know a State Attorney isn't allowed to be involved in anything other than his job for the court. Do you think he is moonlighting for this company or something?"

"Hey, I'm investigating a murder and all bets are on as far as I'm concerned. If Wilson is doing something illegal and the judge found out about it..."

"Okay, I get the picture." Conner handed the folder back to Nick. "Mrs. Ramsey may know more about this. I assume we're going to talk to her as soon as the funeral is behind them."

"As soon as she feels ready to talk to us. I have a feeling she'll be anxious to have the investigation move forward."

Nick looked around once more, then on second thought picked up the trial transcript and put it under his arm before he answered Conner's puzzled look. "Homework. Think I need to bone up on what happened in one of these courtrooms eighteen years ago. Always the possibility the jury got it wrong."

Chapter Ten

By seven o'clock that evening, Nick turned off his computer, threw a half-eaten doughnut he'd called lunch into the trash can, and sent Maureen a text telling her he was on his way. It was a relief to get out of the office. A soft muted evening light illuminated the vivid array of fuchsia, pink, lavender, and white azalea bushes that brightened the spring landscape. Nature's annual floral display lifted Nick's spirits after a sullen day at work, and as he drove along Highway 90 he hummed a tune.

By the time he got to Maureen's condo on Escambia Bay, she was waiting for him on the porch. As she picked up her purse and started down the steps to Nick's car, a gentle breeze off the bay danced with her shoulder-length hair. Nick smiled and a warm fuzzy feeling swept through him. *How I enjoy running my fingers through those silken strands.*

He reached across the gear shift and opened the passenger side door. Maureen barely had time to settle in when he placed an unexpected kiss on her lips and put a bouquet of daises in her hands. Suddenly, she backed off and the flowers fell to the floor.

"Nick, I'm allergic. Daisies are deadly for me. I'm so sorry. That was so sweet of you.

Without hesitation, Nick picked up the bouquet and thrust it out his open window into the grass. "No problem—it was just a little peace offering for being short with you this morning. This case has me wound tight. Be forewarned—you may see another side of me before it's all over."

A tease in Maureen's voice brought a grin to Nick's lips. "You mean I've been dating a man with a façade all these months?" The dimple in her right cheek deepened and she continued, "So…you're admitting you have a human side, huh? And I thought you were the perfect male."

Nick squeezed her hand and his look intensified. "I can assure you I'm not perfect, but I am all male—especially in present company."

In an effort to change the direction of this conversation, Maureen reminded him, "And this female is starving. Head to Milton, Nick. I can smell the catfish now."

* * *

The twenty minute drive to the restaurant went by quickly as the day's traffic no longer consisted of commuters traveling to and from Pensacola. Even though the parking lot at David's Catfish House was full, there was still room for more customers. The clean, homey atmosphere and excellent food always drew crowds.

Nick chuckled to himself as he recalled Maureen's resistance to "Southern Cuisine". It took several attempts to get her to try crawfish and mullet back bones. Now she devoured the hush puppies, coleslaw, catfish and sweet ice tea as though she were a native. *I'll make a Southern gal out of her yet.*

As much as he wanted to keep work out of their conversation, Nick couldn't contain himself. "So did the autopsy reveal anything we didn't already know?"

"From the wounds, we're positive the judge was killed with a shotgun. If it's any solace to you, he didn't linger. Probably never knew what hit him. Andy got some good prints off the boat's railing. I'll send them over tomorrow."

The arrival of the waitress with their order put an end to any further discussion of the autopsy. Besides, both were eager to satisfy their hunger. They were halfway through the meal when Nick made a confession.

"You know I can't keep anything from my AA confidant, don't you?"

Puzzled, Maureen asked, "And what would that be?"

Nick placed his fork on the side of his plate and wiped his mouth with his napkin, "This was one of those days I would have gladly welcomed a stiff drink."

Shock and alarm registered on Maureen's face. "No, Nick, hold on. You've come too far these months to destroy the progress you've made. Not once have you missed a meeting with me."

"Don't worry. You're the reason I've stuck with the program. What would I have done without my accountability partner?" His smile intensified.

"We've helped each other, Nick. I've had my weak moments, too."

"It goes beyond AA, Maureen." Nick reached across the table with one hand and laced his fingers with Maureen's left hand. His voice grew tender and he spoke with true sincerity. "I want to be more than your AA partner. You've brought a spark back into my life. I feel alive again."

Nick searched her eyes for any sign that she felt the same. At first he recognized the twinkle he'd come to adore when she was pleased, then a sudden change came over her.

A chill ran through his heart. Her focus shifted from looking at Nick to glancing over his shoulder. He saw fear in her eyes and she lowered her head.

She wasn't ready for this, he lamented. *I've spoken too soon. She's not ready for a commitment.*

"I'm sorry, Maureen. Me and my big mouth. Poor timing eh? I don't mean to rush you into something you're not ready for. We've got plenty of time. Forgive me."

Tears threatened to spill onto her flushed cheeks and she dabbed at them with her napkin.

"I can't explain my feelings right now, Nick. It's not your fault." She pushed aside the remainder of her dinner. "Can we leave, please?"

"Of course." Nick signaled to the waitress to bring the bill.

They rode back to Maureen's condo in silence. Each buried in their own thoughts. In his usual manner, Nick walked Maureen to the door, opened it, and walked in first to check for intruders. Satisfied all was secure, she followed and put her hand on his arm before she spoke.

"Thank you for dinner. I'd make coffee and invite you to stay, but I really am tired tonight. Will you take a rain check?"

"Of course." It was all Nick could do to keep from reaching for her. He longed to hold this woman in his arms and convince her to trust him—if that was the issue. *Back off,* a small voice whispered. *Now's not the time. Give her some space or you'll lose her for good.*

As he turned to leave, Maureen surprised him by brushing her lips across his cheek. "We'll always be friends, Nick. Goodnight."

Chapter Eleven

The pews in First Baptist Church in Milton overflowed with friends, family, peers, and mourning citizens. Judge Ramsey's life touched everyone from the white-collared professional to the middle class and even the downtrodden.

The scent of a multitude of floral arrangements from the vestibule to the inner sanctuary hung in the air like overpowering perfume. Beside a cherry wood coffin a small table covered in white linen displayed a family Bible, a silver framed photo of Henry Ramsey dressed in his black judge's robe, and a gavel. Nick, Conner, and two other members on the investigative team dispersed and seated themselves among the crowd. Not only were they attending the funeral to show their respect, but it was a known fact that killers got morose satisfaction from seeing the family suffer. In Nick's opinion, his eyes alone were not enough to survey the crowd for suspicious behavior.

As soft, reverent music faded away, the pastor entered through a side door and walked up to the pulpit. A contingent of judges dressed in their official court apparel followed him. They took their place in a reserved area behind the family.

A hush settled over the room and the celebration of Henry Ramsey's life began. Along with appropriate scripture read by the pastor, close friends and peers presented eulogies. A soloist sang, "How Great Thou Art," which ignited another round of sniffles and tears. It was all over in forty-five minutes, and six pallbearers took their positions and escorted the coffin to the waiting hearse.

Because of the extended slow-moving cavalcade of Santa Rosa Deputy patrol cars heading the procession to the cemetery, the drive took over a half hour. Vehicles heading in the opposite direction pulled to the right side of the highway to show respect and folks walking along the sidewalks took one last glimpse of the hearse that carried a man they admired to his final resting place.

At the cemetery, Nick detached himself again from his team and moved along the perimeter of the throng until he stopped near the burial site. His eyes scanned those close by and settled on Samuel Wilson dressed in a pin-striped suit conversing with a group of judges.

Hmm, thought Nick, *word around the Sheriff's Office is that the State Attorney has his eye on a bench seat. Ramsey's death will no doubt hasten that appointment. He looks to me more like a man campaigning for office rather than mourning.*

With the family settled before the coffin, the pastor looked at Samuel Wilson and cleared his throat as a sign to stop talking. Samuel's faced flushed as he nervously straightened his tie and became silent.

The internment was brief. Pastor Tindle offered prayers of comfort to the family and the soloist sang one last song, "'Til We Meet Again."

Nick waited until a trickle of folks gathered around the family before he offered his proper condolences. Glenda Ramsey grasped his hand, her eyes swollen from tears that flowed in unending streams, and whispered in his ear, "Call me tomorrow and we'll arrange a time that's convenient for you to talk. I'm anxious to see my husband's killer brought to justice."

Nick affirmed her request. "We all are, ma'am. I have several questions—a couple that might surprise you."

"Not much surprises an old lady my age, Lieutenant. You know Henry and I were more than husband and wife. From the time we dated as high school sweethearts, we were true confidants. He respected my opinion, and every now and then we discussed difficult cases. Now mind you, what we talked about never left our home. Absolute trust was a cardinal rule. I know there were things Henry never told me for my own protection, but he wanted a woman's perspective, too." A hint of a smile crossed Glena's lips. "There are times when our intuition is correct."

"I don't doubt that for a second." Nick squeezed her hand. "Expect my call."

Chapter Twelve

Early morning traffic slowed Nick's eagerness to begin work this morning and he took several deep breaths to keep his patience while sluggish drivers talked on cell phones, texted, or spent time at a red light putting on makeup. *Women and their vanity*, he sighed. Finally, he turned the wheel of his Camaro into the parking lot and walked with intent into the Sheriff's Office building.

With his obligatory stop in the lounge, he poured a coffee, checked out the doughnuts, decided to pass on the sweets, and went to his office. Once inside, his eyes searched his desk for the finger prints Maureen told him she would send over. Nothing but the file folder concerning the Ramsey case and the Washington trial transcript was evident.

Strange. She told me at dinner that her assistant got some good prints. Nick glanced at his watch. *I'll give her another hour.*

In the meantime, he dialed the Ramsey residence. Sarah answered. After a brief conversation, Nick made an appointment to meet with her and her mother at 2:00 p.m. While he waited for Connor to report in, he picked up the Washington transcript and tried to remember the details of that case.

Otis Washington. Black man. Soft spoken and always friendly. Yes, now I recall how surprised I was that he was recognized as the highjacker. Dad and I always launched his boat in the Blackwater Bay at Otis's fish camp. He had a twin brother, too. Cocky guy with an attitude. Street smart. Wonder what happened to him? I don't believe he was even present at the trial.

Before Nick got much further into the transcript, his partner ambled into the office. One look at Conner's bloodshot eyes and drooping shoulders told the story.

"Tell me it's against the sheriff's policy for anyone to come to work with less than five hours sleep. Please send me home or better yet, let me take the lounge for about two more hours. See ya at noon."

Nick couldn't resist the chance to needle this new father. "You wimp. A big guy like you who I've seen take down some of the toughest out there and you're telling me your little eight-pound son has you looking like you've been hung over for three days."

"You had to be there, partner. Every hour for twenty minutes he'd double up his tiny legs, turn beet red, and scream his lungs out. I tell you, this colic is torture—for him and the parents. The doctor tells us most babies grow out of it in three months. Hope I last that long." Conner wiped his brow and sighed.

"Go get yourself a coffee. I left a chocolate doughnut for you, too. Take your time and try to get up to speed because we're meeting with Sarah and her mother at 2:00. Sure hope we get something solid to get this ball rolling. I don't relish the thought of the governor breathing down our necks."

Conner started out the door. "That's enough to get my blood moving." For an instant he stopped and looked back. "Chocolate, right? My favorite doughnut. Now, that's the kind of partner who has your back. Thanks, pal."

* * *

As Nick continued to read the transcript, an unsettling feeling about the trial stirred unanswered questions. *Why wasn't an APB put out on Otis Washington's twin brother? Where was Owen when all the action came down? Who did the baseball cap with the 'Blackwater Fish Camp" patch on the front really belong to?*

It was tempting to finish reading as the trial unfolded with each page, but Nick had another case on his mind that took priority. He picked up the phone and dialed forensics. Andy's familiar voice answered. Nick wasted no time with small talk . "Andy. I'm looking for the prints you took off the judge's party barge. Maureen told me she'd have them on my desk today and I don't see them anywhere."

"Let me take a look in the outgoing box. We've had a busy week. Hang on."

Within seconds, Andy returned. "They're here, all right. Never left the office. I'll bring them over myself."

"That's not like your boss. She's usually 'Johnny on the spot.' Is she around? I need to talk to her?"

"Sorry. You missed her by about five minutes. Some guy came to the office and the next thing I know she tells me she's taking an early lunch and boom she's gone. Never even introduced me to him."

Nick's stomach gave a lurch. "What'd he look like?"

"Tall, dark hair, good looking fellow. Kinda like one of those male models you see in the magazines."

Nick felt his body heat start to rise and jealousy reared its ugly head. *Another man, eh? So that could explain her cool behavior the other night.*

Trying not to show his hand, Nick ended the conversation. "Thanks, Andy. Try to get those prints to me as soon as possible, okay?"

"I'm on my way, Lieutenant."

Chapter Thirteen

Owen Washington woke up with a hangover. His head ached and he felt his stomach churn. *I need some* weed, he muttered. *Gotta puke. It's the only thing to stop this nauseous feeling. Don't know why it's not legal. Dumb.* He reached across the bed to waken his woman to go get him his drugs, but instead, he felt the cold, cotton sheet—not the warm, naked body he expected. A look of disgust added to his distress. *Out shoppin' again.*

He swung his legs off the mattress and placed them on the floor. Careful not to move too quickly, he sat on the edge of the bed with his head between his legs. *Where had he hid his stash this time? Oh, yeah, there ain't none left. Used it all last night at the party. Gotta make another run to Mobile. It's time Sam'll be needin' a refill, anyway. And I needs the money. Lord o' mercy this gal of mine can spend it.*

Another wave of nausea sent him into the bathroom where the sound of retching broke the silence. No sooner had Owen washed his face and started to look for his clothes when he heard the familiar jingle on his cell phone. He glanced at the screen and recognized the number.

"Yeah, Mr. State Attorney what's up?"

"How's your supply? My friend from up north likes your stuff and wants more. You met him last week. He was impressed with your style and has another job for you. Interested?"

"What is it?"

"Can't talk now. Not on the phone, so find us another spot. Your brother really messed up our meeting place. Hey, didn't see you at the funeral yesterday. Afraid to show your face?"

Owen sensed this conversation going in a different direction. "Why you ask me that? Judge Ramsey meant nothin' to me, dead or alive."

"Just giving you a little warning. You could be a suspect. A case could be made that after all these years guilt caught up with you. To make amends to your brother, who you know took the rap for you, you killed the judge who put him away."

"You ain't in court now, Sam, so you can stop playin' with my mind." Owen's hands trembled and he almost dropped the phone.

"You're right." Sam paused a moment before lowering the boom, "But I could sure make a convincing case in front of a jury if I had to."

The warning to Owen did not go unnoticed. "And I have a few tales of my own to tell, so I guess we're even. Like my mama used to say, 'Owen, sooner or later ya sins is gonna find you out. Guess we's both bin lucky.'"

"Can't argue with that, so get back in touch with me. My friend doesn't like to wait."

* * *

Nick looked up from the transcript when he heard a knock on his door. "C'mon in," he yelled.

Andy appeared with a folder containing the prints. He spread them out on Nick's desk and the two men examined them.

"Clean," observed Nick. "Nice job, pal. Now we have a crucial element in this case."

"Thanks, Nick. Just a part of the job. Makes it easier on everyone. Let's hope NCIC has them on their data base."

"If our killer is a repeater, his prints will be there. Let's get them over to Amber. Maybe we can catch her before she goes to lunch."

As they walked down the hallway, Nick casually asked, "Maureen get back yet?"

"Not to my knowledge. Sure was strange the way she up and left with no explanation."

"Well, I'm sure she had her reason," Nick tried to sound convincing. "Say, if you don't mind, tell her to go ahead to our AA meeting tonight. I may be running late."

"No problem. I need to get back. Good luck on the prints."

Amber met Nick as she placed the key to her office into the lock. "I know," she teased, "you need these to go into the main data base like yesterday." She unlocked the door and took the folder from Nick.

"You've got it, Amber. But I'll give you a break. Go to lunch. They can wait another hour. Anyway, I have an appointment coming up soon, so I'll drop by then. Deal?"

An infectious smile lit up her face. "Deal. My boyfriend's waiting."

Chapter Fourteen

At exactly 2:00 p.m. Nick and Conner drove onto the circular driveway in front of the Ramsey residence. A breeze off Blackwater Bay whistled through the wisteria and redbud trees that surrounded the home and left the refreshing scent of spring.

The detectives met Sarah at the door and she ushered them into a family room that offered a picturesque view of the water. Glenda, stoic and dignified, looked every inch the Southern lady from her perfectly coiffed white hair and black dress to the stunning circle of cultured pearls that hung around her neck. She started to rise when Nick assured her it wasn't necessary. Both men took a seat across from her on a spacious couch.

"Gentlemen, can I offer you some refreshment? Lemonade, water, soda?"

Both men declined and Nick took out his notepad and pen then started the questioning.

"Ma'am…"

Before he could continue, Glenda interrupted. "Lieutenant, I know you were raised to be a polite lad, but please call me Glenda. It's just less formal and we've known you since Sarah was a teenager.

"Indeed, that's true." Nick smiled at the daughter who held her mother's hand. " Whatever you wish. Now let me warn you that some of our questions may be very personal and cause you to tear up. Don't hold back on our account, okay?"

Satisfied that Glenda was ready to open up, Nick began. "I know that judges routinely get threats, but has there been any recent activity of that sort?" Nick looked at Sarah and advised, "Sarah, feel free to jump in at any time. There may be something you know that your mom has forgotten."

"Yes, you're correct about the threats." Glenda agreed. "Over the years they came in any manner or fashion from letters to late night calls, and once a rattlesnake ended up in our mailbox. The poor mailman killed it and warned me to be careful. Remember that, Sarah?"

Her daughter nodded and added, "There was also that time when a plot to blow up father's car was discovered. Vengeance is what folks are after. For some reason or another the verdict didn't please them and they blamed my dad."

Conner joined the conversation. "Anything in the last six months?"

"Yes, now that I think about it," returned Glenda. "There was a custody case involving drug-addicted parents and a four-year-old girl. They were making meth in their trailer and it caught fire."

"We're aware of that situation," cut in Conner. "Lucky a patrol car was in the neighborhood and he called 911. The parents tried to make a run for it, but he saw them. They left the child standing in the yard crying and scared to death."

Glenda shook her head in disgust.

"The letter Henry received threatened him with his life if the little girl was taken from them. In the end, my husband gave custody to the grandparents." Glenda went on to voice her opinion. "Isn't it a shame nowadays so many grandparents must take responsibility for their grandchildren. What has happened to this generation?"

Nick realized it was a rhetorical question, but he needed more information about the threat.

"Glenda, do you know what happened to the letter?"

She leapt to her feet and blurted out, "It's here, in a file that Henry kept in case some angry soul made good on his threat. I'd have some proof if it was needed in court." A tear escaped and rolled down her cheek. "I guess I may, won't I?"

"I'd like to read it, Glenda," said Nick. "Maybe it's a hoax, maybe not?"

"It's in his den. I'll get it."

Sarah noticed a stagger in her mother's gait and she jumped up to steady her. "I'll help you look, Mama."

While the women retrieved the letter, Nick penned the information gathered so far. He scanned the questions he intended to ask and one stood out. It was personal and he needed to phrase it so that it tied into the case.

Within minutes, Sarah handed Nick a lined sheet of paper used in school binders. The writing was uneven and the spelling phonetic.

"I made you a copy. I'd like to keep the original," Sarah commented.

"No problem."

Glenda returned to her seat and Nick continued, "Conner and I have already been to the court house to check out the judge's chamber. Two items caught our attention."

"Oh, what were they?" asked Sarah. Both women looked at Nick with curiosity.

"One was a trial transcript of a case that Henry handled eighteen years ago. They released the victim last week. He may have been innocent."

Sarah was quick to pick upon the insinuation. "Are you telling us it's possible father died because someone wanted revenge?"

Conner stepped in with his comment. "It's happened before. The convicted feel they've been wronged, and over the years it turns to bitterness and an urge to get even. At this point it's supposition. Another probable suspect."

"You said you found two items?" questioned Glenda.

Nick took a deep breath and dived in. "The other was a folder with the title, 'Worldwide Investments' written on the cover. I'm very cautious about crossing the line between what's business and what's personal, so please understand because of the nature of what I found inside, it created some questions." Nick stopped to let this information sink into Glenda's weary mind.

"Go on, Nick. I'm curious too, but I believe I can shed some light on this for you. Don't be concerned about privacy. You know I trust you."

Nick smiled and continued, "Apparently, Henry had some business with this company, but he didn't agree with the annual report and the calculations, according to the notes he wrote on the side of the paper. At the back of the folder was a copy of a letter he'd written to the Security and Exchange Commission asking for a review of Worldwide Investments."

Glenda nodded her head as Nick continued to talk.

"What intrigued me as well was a note attached to the folder that indicated he'd scheduled a meeting with Samuel Wilson. That meeting took place a week before Henry's death. Did you know about all this?"

Glenda spoke right up. "Yes. Let me back up about three years ago and fill in some of the blanks. Henry was very conscientious when it came to saving money for his retirement. You may know that a state pension will not make you a wealthy man." Glenda paused and her face flushed as though she hesitated to admit, "Henry was a wonderful man in so many areas of his life, but he was human, after all, and don't we all have a little bit of greed inside of us?"

The detectives listened with rapt attention. He leaned in closer.

"Samuel Wilson convinced my husband to invest several thousand dollars in this Worldwide Investments. He swore up and down there was no way we could lose a penny. He told us the president and founder of the company was his friend from Harvard Law School. Top of his class. Came from a well-known respected family. Samuel even showed Henry his own statements. Told him that's what helped him buy that beach house out on Santa Rosa Island."

Nick's face took on a bewildered look and he used his hand as a signal for Glenda to stop.

"Excuse me, but I need to get something straight. It was my understanding that a State Attorney is not allowed to represent a company if he or she is an employee of the court. Am I correct?"

"You are right. Henry questioned Samuel about his involvement. He assured us he was simply passing on a personal tip and there was no compensation made to him.

"For the first couple years, we earned a decent return, but a couple months ago when the financial reports arrived, something about the figures seemed amiss. The earnings were not there. Henry met with Samuel to tell him he'd written to the Securities and Exchange Commission and asked for an investigation. Samuel wasn't able to provide a reasonable explanation about the returns and stormed out of the office. As far as I know, Henry hasn't received any word yet from the SEC."

Sarah's face turned pale and she faced her mother.

"Mama, you never told me this was going on. This company may have swindled you out of retirement money. And if the SEC is doing an investigation, somebody at the top of Worldwide Investments is not going to be happy. I see why you're pursuing this line of thought, Nick."

"Please call me if anyone tries to get in touch with you, Glenda," advised Nick.

"Do you feel safe, Mrs. Ramsey?" asked Conner. "We can have a patrol car sweep the area every night if you'd like."

A smile on Glenda's face revealed the thankfulness she felt. "No, that's not necessary. My son-in-law has already assured me he won't let anyone hurt me. Daniel's got things under control. But I do appreciate your offer."

With that, Nick and Conner stood, gave both Glenda and Sarah a compassionate hug, and excused themselves with a promise to keep the family informed of any new developments.

Like a kid anxious for Christmas, he couldn't wait to get back to the office to see if data from the National Crime Information Center revealed the identity of the prints.

Chapter Fifteen

"Bingo!" Amber's voice sounded triumphant the moment Nick walked into her office. "You may have your man. She handed over a sheet of paper.

One look at the photo and the expression on Nick's face turned from anticipation to disappointment.

Amber asked, "What's wrong? I thought you'd be pleased to get this information. It's a major clue in the investigation, isn't it?"

"Yes, but I was hoping it'd be someone else. I know this man, or I thought I did. Thanks, sweetie. Well done as usual."

Otis, Otis, why? This thought kept repeating itself like a broken car alarm as Nick walked over to Conner's office.

"You're gonna tell Kendall?" asked his partner. "This is a big deal."

"Of course I will, but not today. First, I want to finish reading the transcript of Otis's trial. So far, there are plenty of holes in that case—at least the way I see it. First thing tomorrow morning, I'm going to take you to a fish camp to have a little chat with the owner. Besides, it's time for home and I have some reading to do." Nick turned to leave then stopped. His lips curled into a grin as he looked at Conner.

"Hey, pal, try using earplugs tonight. See ya."

* * *

Nick popped a soda, sat in his Lay-Z-Boy, and dialed Maureen's number. He told himself he was not keeping tabs on her personal activities. Just wanted to keep her in the loop and tell her the prints belonged to Otis. But he knew better. In fact, his pulse raced and his body heat accelerated when he pictured her with another man.

The phone rang over and over, but there was no response. *Oh well, I'll see her at the meeting tonight.* Nick glanced at his watch and took a long swig of soda. *Better get going. Evening traffic is going to be tough.*

The AA speaker was ten minutes into his talk when Nick walked into the room. Familiar faces greeted him as he surveyed the circle. One face was missing. *Where is she? She's never missed a meeting. Did Andy forget to tell her to drive on ahead of him tonight? I've already called and there was no answer.*

It was difficult concentrating on what the speaker was saying. Every few seconds he heard a word or two but he had difficulty connecting the dots. The only comprehensive thought in Nick's mind was, *where are you, Maureen?*

Finally, a round of applause signaled the end of the talk and Nick bolted from his chair and raced to his car. His fingers fumbled with the keypad on his phone and he had to redial. Still no answer. *Get over it,* his head told him as he drove home. *Get over it. She's not your wife. Besides, wasn't that one of the reasons you're divorced? Too controlling.*

Defeated, Nick settled in for the night. He had three more pages of the transcript to finish when his phone rang. Eager to hear Maureen's voice, he picked up on the first ring.

"Hi, Dad," the sweet sound of his daughter's words crushed his expectation.

"Oh, hi, honey." Silence followed as Nick's mind changed gears.

"Dad, you okay? That's not your usual greeting. Hard day at work?"

"You might say so. Working on Judge Ramsey's murder. I'm sure the news reached the Keys."

"Sure did. I heard it on the news. Too bad. He kept a lot of lowlife off the streets." Changing subjects, Penny asked, "Did you get the shirt I sent you? Wasn't the slogan cool? 'Nothin' greater than a Gator!'"

"Thanks, Penny." replied Nick with a lack of enthusiasm. "I'll save it for the opening season."

Penny changed the subject again. "Dad, something's not right. I can hear it in your voice and don't tell me it's work because you've had lots of important cases, so 'fess up. It's your daughter on this end."

A long sigh from Nick echoed its way through the airways. "Okay. Something's going on with Maureen. Without any warning she's changed."

"What do you mean changed? Did you say something to tick her off? You know it didn't take much to set mom in that direction?"

"Not that I recall. I'm really trying, honey, with this relationship. I don't want to lose her, but she's acting strange. Not answering my calls. She even missed our regular AA meeting tonight, and that's never happened in almost a year."

"I can only give you a female perspective, Dad, but don't jump the gun. I know she cares for you—anyone can see that. You've been happier than I've ever known. Women need their space sometimes. She's had trauma in her life and maybe she's afraid because you're a cop you'll get taken down and leave her, too. If you love her, be patient."

"Oh, I do love this woman and I'm trying to keep calm. But you know you'll always be my first love, Penny. Take care and thanks for calling. Good night, sweetheart."

Chapter Sixteen

The bad news came from the dispatcher the minute Nick walked into the Sheriff's Office building.

"Nick, wait up a minute. A call came in a few minutes ago that I think you need to know about."

"This early in the morning. Must be important. What's it all about, Marie?"

"Come into my cubicle and listen to the recording. Of course, I have no idea how legitimate it is. But we take 'em all, don't we?"

Marie found the call on her recorder and turned up the volume. After Marie's "Sheriff's Office—how can I help you?" a man's deep, rough voice started the conversation.

"I'm callin' about the judge's killin'. The night he was shot, me and my buddies drove down to the Blackwater and was fixin' to put our boat in at that ole fish camp when a black guy stopped us with his shotgun. He looked like he was ready to git in his boat when he heard us pull in. Out he comes, pointin' the gun and demandin' money. Said he owned the place and it cost ten bucks to use his launch.

"I ain't never seen him around there before and I've been fishin' out of that camp for twelve years. Looked awful suspicious to us, 'specially when the poor judge was shot that night. Bet they're gonna find it was a 12 gauge shot gun that killed him."

"What is your name, sir? The detectives may contact you."

"Benny T. Barnell, ma'am. I don't have no phone so they's gonna haf to find me at my brother's garage. I'm a mechanic over there at Barnell's on Highway 90. We work on lots of them patrol cars so they know where to find me."

"I'll see that Detective Melino gets the message, sir. Goodbye."

Nick finished writing down the caller's name and said,

"Thanks, Marie. We'll check it out. Oh, Conner and I are going out for most of the morning should the sheriff or anyone else need to see us."

Nick pondered the call as he poured his coffee and walked down the hall to his office. He drained the last of his brew just as his partner walked in and planted himself in one of the chairs. His face looked rested and there was a sparkle in his eyes. "It worked, my friend. I got some sleep last night. Can't you tell?"

Nick looked up from the sports section of the morning paper. "What worked?"

"The ear plugs you advised me to wear."

"You mean for once you seriously took my advice? There's hope for you yet, Connor."

"Of course, it came with a price." A guilty look replaced Conner's joy.

"How's that?"

"Heather's not speaking to me this morning. She tells me she spent most of the night rocking our little son."

"A dozen roses will fix that, my friend. Guaranteed."

* * *

The drive out to the fish camp brought back memories to Nick of all the times he and his dad fished the Blackwater. He missed those times since his father died. It just wasn't the same without his parent telling him how to maneuver the boat or troll for fish as though he were still a young child. Of course, not all days were full of fun. Nick knew that on the first of every month when his dad got paid, he'd pull a bottle of booze out of his pack where he'd hidden it from his mother. His drunken state never made his father nasty. He simply sat at the bow of the boat, cushioned his head, and fell asleep. Nick used this time to explore the river. He memorized every inlet and bay. Even now, he visualized the exact spot where Henry Ramsey met his death.

Nick broke the silence as they drove down a sandy lane shaded on each side by pine and oak trees. "Sure hope Otis hasn't gone out for the day's catch yet. I still have a gut feeling he's not the one we're after and I don't want him to bolt."

"But," cut in Connor, "the evidence is stacking up. Prints, motive, now possible witnesses that he owns a shotgun. Doesn't look good."

A sign nailed to a decaying tree and written in red paint caught the men's attention.

Stop! Please read. Private property.
Washington Fish Camp
$10.00 launch fee. Pay up front.

Nick slowly drove his Camaro through an opening in the fence and stopped beside a small, wooden frame cabin. The detectives got out and looked around. A black man dressed in overalls stood beside a fish cleaning table at the water's edge.

"Be with you fellers in a minute," shouted Otis. "Need to dump these fish guts in the river. Got a pet turtle looks for 'em every mornin'."

Nick and Connor sauntered over to where the smell of rotting fish was the strongest. Houseflies swarmed around the table and Otis took several swats at them, only to have them return. With his chore completed, he looked at his visitors.

"You men meanin' to fish today? Don't look to me like you're dressed for it. Where's your boat?"

Nick took the lead. "Otis Washington?"

"Yes, sir."

"I'm Lieutenant Nick Melino and this is my partner, Sergeant Connor Andrews."

Otis's body changed from a loose casual posture to a stiff, defiant stance. He stood searching Nick's face then pointed a finger at him.

"You that cop that arrested me eighteen years ago. Used to come here with your daddy. Now whatcha want? I ain't done nothin'."

"That's right, Otis. Is there someplace we can talk? How 'bout your porch out of the sun?"

Otis said not a word but lead the way up to the cabin. He motioned for the men to sit in two straight-back chairs while he took a stool.

Nick saw the flickering of the man's chocolate colored fearful eyes, the drawn lips, and his trembling hands. *I need to get him to relax,* thought Nick, *or he'll clam up. Start with what's familiar to him.*

"I remember how much Dad and I enjoyed coming here to launch our boat. So, how's the fishing this spring?"

"Pretty decent. I catch my fill every day. My diet's pretty limited but suits me. Flounder, mullet, bream. I eat 'em all."

Connor figured out Nick's ploy and joined in. "Business good? We read the sign."

"Keeps me in groceries. 'Course you fellas know I've bin gone a few years and folks don't know I'm back. I reckon there's bin a whole lot of trespassin' while I's away. That gonna change. Had to run a car load of 'em off the other night."

Hmm, so the call to dispatch was true. Nick needed to dig further.

"Otis, I have to tell you something and you may not believe me, but I mean it. I read the transcript of your trial recently and something tells me you went to prison an innocent man."

Instantly, a change of demeanor came over this man. He stared at Nick and his eyes became pools of liquid. He reached out for Nick's hand and his face softened.

"You means it, sir? No one in all these years believed me. I didn't highjack that woman's car and kill her child."

"Tell us what happened," urged Connor.

Otis took a deep breath, wiped the wetness from his cheeks, and began to unravel his side of the story.

"It weren't no floundering that night on account of the weather. Rained all day. Most folks don't like getting' wet you know. Makes it hard on my business, but that's how it goes in a fish camp. Some days is good. Others ain't worth a plug nickel."

Nick sensed the financial struggle this man faced each day.

Otis continued, "But I never bin afraid of no rain, so I left the camp about seven when all that carjackin' was goin' on and stayed out a good part of the night. Since no one saw me out there, I had no alibi. Why'd you come after me, Lieutenant? As I remember, you took me in the next mornin'. What proof you have?"

"The woman in the car saw a black man wearing a cap with your camp name written on it. He was the driver. She also swore that the other man on the passenger's side yelled at the assailant, "Washington, hurry up. We gotta get out of here!"

"Your name is Washington and your camp was well known in those days. When I brought you in, she identified you out of a lineup. I had my doubts it was you because I thought I knew the kind of man you are. But the evidence pointed at you, Otis. What bothers me is that I knew you had a twin brother, but he was nowhere to be seen and Samuel Wilson wasn't interested in finding him."

At the mention of Wilson's name Otis stiffened. "He was trying to make a name for himself and convince a jury to send anyone to prison. I was another notch in his belt. I heard in prison he finally made it to State Attorney. And that lawyer the court gived me was straight outta college—wet behind the ears. I don't think he believed me either."

"Otis, I have to ask you some difficult questions concerning your attitude toward Judge Ramsey and what happened to him the other night. You know someone shot him?"

Fear once again took hold of Otis and his eyes danced from one side to the other.

"Yes, sir, I do, but it weren't me? It looks bad. Makes sense that after all those lonely years in prison I'd want to take revenge for my sentence. Oh, I'll admit I thought about it, but you know what stopped me?"

"Tell us," urged Connor.

"My Mama's words. She was a fine Christian woman. Bless her heart, she with Papa and the Lawd now. But she always quotin' scripture and many times she tell Owen and me, 'Justice is mine, sayeth the Lawd.'"

Again tears ran down Otis's ebony face, but he wasn't finished.

"Four nights ago, I took my boat out on the bay for the first time in eighteen years. I needed fish for food, so I had to go. It was getting close to dark and I set my anchor in one of the bays not too far off Peterson's point. I loves that time of night. Everything quiet. Not much breeze. All of a sudden two shots rang out around the bend from where I was fishing. I'm thinkin'—coon huntin'. Somebody's after the coon. But a dog gets to barkin' and for fifteen minutes he never stopped. I knows that no coon huntin' dog. Somebody's in trouble, so I took off to look. When I turned the bend, I saw the night lights on a party barge and a body slumped over the steering wheel. I pulled up alongside and tied my boat to one of the railings, then jumped aboard and ran over to the man. When I turned his body over, I saw who it was. No question he was dead. Limp and blood drippin' on the dog and on the barge."

"What did you do then? Go home?"

"No, I couldn't leave him all night like that, so I went down to the marina 'bout a mile away and told them to call 911. I's scared, Lieutenant. I knew the police would accuse me of killin' the judge since I just served my time. Is that why you're here? To arrest me again?"

Nick broke the news, "Forensics lifted your prints off the railing."

This time Otis broke down. His face shone with the new flood of tears and a low growl erupted from within his shaking body. With his hands in a praying position, his head looked upward, and he bellowed, "Sweet Jesus, don't let them take me away again."

Nick and Connor remained quiet and let the storm pass. Finally, Nick reached over and touched Otis's arm.

"Listen to me, man. I believe you and I make you this promise." Otis stooped over and this time put his head between his knees as Nick continued, "I'm going to work to clear your name from the carjacking. But first, I'm going to talk to Sheriff Kendall and try and get a judge to allow you to remain in house arrest. You'll have to appear in court for a hearing, but I'll be with you. I'm going to try and keep you out of jail."

Otis looked in disbelief at Nick. "You do that for me? Why?"

"I know I'm putting myself on the line, but I learned a few things from Judge Ramsey. You see, he and I were good friends. He had a heart for mankind and tried to see the good in everyone. How many times did you help me with my drunken father when he couldn't even get out of the boat on his own two feet? Never did you talk around town about him, either."

"Your father was a good man, Lieutenant He took to the bottle to forget the death of your brother. You knows he blamed himself for sendin' him to the store when a crazy kid was holdin' up the place. Don't be shamed of him."

"I understand my father's behavior more now than I ever did growing up. I picked up his drinking habits to try and solve some of my own problems, but because of a very good friend, I've got a handle on them now. AA has helped a lot." Nick chuckled. "I don't know how we got off track, but if I help you, you've got to make a promise to me, too."

"What's that?"

"You can't leave this fish camp. There's no running away. Understand—if you try, you'll show yourself a liar and I'll be in big trouble."

"I promise, Lieutenant Nick." With that, a black and a white hand shook on a deal.

* * *

Back in the car, Connor looked at Nick and said, "I can't believe what I just saw. You really believe he's innocent, don't you."

"Haven't you ever had a gut feeling and it turned out you were right? If it hadn't been the fact that I grew up with this man every Saturday morning and saw how he treated people, I wouldn't have gone out on a limb. It tore me up when I put the cuffs on him the first time. But I went along with the State Attorney because I was a rookie detective and didn't have the courage to rock the boat. Experience has taught me the law—or those pretending to represent the law—are not always right. How would you like to have eighteen years of your life taken away because some self-promoting assistant to the State Attorney wanted to move up the ladder? Wilson didn't do his job."

Connor knew Nick was on a roll and he asked, "Where are we going? I thought the road turned north."

"To the marina. I want to talk to the guys who made that call to dispatch. Besides, it will make you feel better about Otis's story if we get a confirmation of the facts. Am I right?"

"You know how to read me, partner."

"I should, after ten years." Nick laughed. "Kinda like a marriage, huh?"

"Please, let's not go there. I still have to pick up some roses."

The marina did a brisk business and today customers kept the staff hopping. After fifteen minutes, one of the owners walked up to the detectives and asked, "You guys need some help?"

"Actually we do," said Nick pulling out his I.D. "Could we talk privately?"

Surprised by the visit, Alex called out to his partner. "Hey, Mike, c'mon over here a minute." Connor flashed his badge.

"We in some kind of trouble?" Mike's head moved from one detective to the other.

"No," came a unified response.

"We can talk in the office," offered Alex.

With the door closed, Nick took the lead. "We're investigating the Ramsey murder case. I understand a black man stopped by here shortly after dark and told you to call 911 that a party barge had a lone dead man aboard."

"Yes, sir, he did and we called immediately. He didn't seem to want to come in under the lights, so I wouldn't be able to recognize him. Took off pretty quick."

"Yeah," chimed in Mike. "That's the same night one of our kayaks got ripped off. Don't suppose you've got time to track that loser down, eh?"

Alex turned to his partner and chided, "Mike, I told you, it's bound to happen. These guys are looking for a killer, not a thief."

"Hey," Connor encouraged, "tell us the details. We might hear something that could help you."

"Okay," Alex began. "Just before sunset this black dude comes in and wants to rent a kayak. Pays in cash. We insist on customers filling out a form—name, address, phone, email—so if it's damaged or is late returning we can contact them."

"Sounds reasonable," added Nick.

Alex took his turn. "I looked this guy over pretty good 'cause he sure didn't look like kayaking was his favorite sport.

Designer clothes, braided hair, and what really caught my eye was the bracelet he was wearing."

Nick's ears perked up. "Why? Did it seem unusual?"

"It was made of gold links and had a medic alert symbol on it. My kid is allergic to peanuts and he has to wear one, too. Course nothing that looked like his. I told him about Erin and asked about his medic alert. Told me he has diabetes. He signed the paper and took off with the kayak on the back of his truck. We haven't seen either one of them since. I checked out the paperwork—all a fraud. Dang, I hate to have to make an insurance claim. All that paperwork. Why can't folks be honest?"

"Then I'd be out a job," joked Nick. He gave Mike a friendly slap on the back. Say, what color is it? Any distinguishing marks?"

Alex piped up. "Lime green with our Blackwater Marina logo on the side."

"We'll keep our ear to the ground. Thanks for your time. You've verified some facts for us." Nick and Connor shook hands in gratitude and left the marina.

"Okay, so Otis's story checks out with those guys. You think Kendall's going to buy it? I'm still hung up on the prints." Connor's argument hung between the two.

Nick became serious. "Listen, Otis may be uneducated, but he's not stupid. After spending eighteen years in among some of the worst offenders and con men behind bars, you think he didn't learn a few of their tricks? If he killed the judge, he sure wouldn't have been sloppy enough to leave his prints. On the other hand, if his human instincts told him a man was in trouble and needed help, his only concern was to get on that boat the best way he could, even if it meant grabbing onto the railing. Remember, he had no idea it was Judge Ramsey at this point."

Connor looked at Nick and softened his stance. "You're starting to make sense. Let's hope Kendall sees it your way."

"Won't know 'til we try." Nick pushed down on the accelerator and his Camaro left a cloud of dust behind them.

Chapter Seventeen

Sheriff Kendall looked up from a massive stack of paperwork as his two senior detectives knocked then entered his office.

"Hey, good timing. I was about to call you. Tallahassee's been on the phone already wanting some details about the investigation. Told them you were on the case working hard and that we'd keep them informed. Now, tell me I didn't perjure myself." An attempt at levity brought a smile to his lips.

Nick cleared his throat and began his argument to help Otis.

"We have made some progress. Forensics lifted prints from the barge and NCIC showed a match to Otis Washington."

Kendall jumped in. "That's the man who was released last week, right? Well, where is he? You've brought him in, haven't you?"

Connor's face flushed and Nick stood his ground. "No, sir, we haven't."

Kendall's reaction was swift and his six-foot frame stood up, his eyes wide with amazement and his voice authoritative. "What? We've got condemning evidence and the man's running around free. What more do you want? A signed confession.?"

"We just came from his fish camp and listened to his story. Yes, the prints belong to Otis, but hear me out. Please."

Sheriff Kendall motioned to Connor to close the door, wiped his brow and went eyeball to eyeball with Nick.

"It better be good, Lieutenant."

Nick started with Otis's clean, upstanding character as he knew him before he served his sentence. Nick then explained the reasons he believed the man was framed. Finally he relayed the events that unfolded the night of the murder that resulted in Otis's prints on the party barge.

Sheriff Kendall shifted his weight in his seat and every now and then his brows knit together as though he wrestled with whether to believe what Nick revealed.

Giving Nick a break, Connor completed the morning's events.

"The owners at the marina told us the same story. Matches word for word."

Silence hung heavy in the air and Nick felt as though he were in a poker game waiting for the last player to show his hand. His breathing grew shallow and he realized the stakes were high. If Kendall refused to allow him to go to a judge for a house arrest warrant the whole deal he made with Otis was useless. Bail, if allowed, would be so high it was not even on the table. Nick lowered his head and his mute prayer asked for a chance to help lift the burden from Otis's shoulders.

Like ice released from its bondage, Kendall's words gave the detectives hope.

"Nick, we've worked together for many years and to my knowledge you've never abused the law or your authority. This is a very unusual request, especially since this case is top priority, but as you know, the final decision is not in my hands but a judge's. However, judges take our recommendations seriously. I'm going to give you a green light. If you're turned down, I want to see Otis Washington in the county jail tomorrow. Understood?"

Tension drained from Nick's body and he held out his hand to shake Kendall's. They had a deal.

* * *

It was late afternoon by the time the detectives had their request on paper and stood before Judge Allen in his chamber. He read it silently then looked at Nick.

"You know what you're asking is very risky, and considering the high profile of Judge Ramsey, it has the potential to blow up in your face. The finger print match is enough to lock Mr. Washington up immediately.

Nick nodded and waited for the answer.

"I'm sorry, Lieutenant, but I need to give this matter considerable thought. Bring the man in tomorrow and I'll have my answer." Judge Allen closed the folder, clasped his hands together, and gave this advice. "If I were you, I wouldn't let Otis Washington out of your sight tonight. See you at 9:00 a.m. sharp.

Neither Connor nor Nick said a word as they descended the courthouse steps and climbed into the car. Each man felt the pressure of the upcoming judge's verdict.

Trying to put a positive spin on the situation, Connor commented. "Well…he could have flat refused. At least it came across to me that he's willing to give it some thought."

"Yeah, it's just that I hate to wait. You know how impatient I can be. The strain on Nick's face echoed in his voice. "I guess I better do what he suggested and keep an eye on Otis tonight."

"How are going to pull that off?"

"When I drop you at work, I'm going home and dig out my camping gear. It's been a while since I've slept in a sleeping bag, but what better way to keep watch. Otis doesn't know it yet, but he's going to have a house guest tonight."

Chapter Eighteen

The smell of fried mullet set Nick's stomach to rumbling as he ambled up to the back porch of Otis's cabin.

Hunched over an old Coleman cook stove, Otis used a slotted spoon to carefully drain the excess bubbling grease off the golden hush puppies.

He looked up as Nick asked, "Say, what does a man have to do to get a meal around here?"

Startled to see the law for the second time in one day, Otis searched Nick's countenance for any clue that might indicate whether this was an official visit or a casual one.

Since Nick was alone, he chose the latter. "There's always room for one more at my table. Pull yourself up a chair. I likes to eat outside and feast my eyes on the river that gives me my vittles. Now, I know from the past that you'll eat any fish that comes out of that water."

A hearty laugh from Nick dissolved any tension between them "You got that right. I remember many the time you wrapped up a fillet or two and instructed me to take them home to my mama. I have to confess, Otis, they didn't always get there. 'Course I never told her they were meant for her."

"Shame on you, boy."

Otis turned off the stove and handed a plate mounded with fish and hush puppies to Nick before his curiosity got the better of him.

"Why you here again, Nick? The Sheriff say no?"

Nick waited until he swallowed his first mouthful of tender, seasoned mullet before answering.

"Good news, my friend. He allowed me to plead with the judge for a house arrest. The judge would not make a decision today. He's not willing to go out on a limb without careful consideration. Even the Governor is weighing in on this one."

Otis sighed and pushed his fish to one side of his plate. "I should never have bothered to check out that boat. None of this would've happened. Wish now I stayed where I was. Somebody would have found the judge next morning."

Nick saw the light of hope fade from this man's face.

"No. You did the right thing. Where's that faith your mama taught you? My team will not give up until we find the killer. Hang in there. By the way, I brought my sleeping bag. I'm staying with you tonight. Tomorrow morning, you and I are going to see Judge Allen. He will probably ask you some questions. Please, be honest. I'm counting on you walking out of there wearing a GPS ankle bracelet."

The hardness in Otis's expression began to relax and he picked up his fork.

"And one more thing." Nick noticed Otis wasn't eating. "Don't let those fillets go to waste. *That* would be a crime."

* * *

For the next hour, a comfortable exchange of conversation went on between the two men. When the sun bid the earth adieu, a new moon peeked through the Spanish moss that hung from the oaks surrounding the cabin.

Nick felt the time was ripe to explore more facts concerning the car hijacking, so he opened up the subject.

"Otis, do you still have the bracelet that was shown in court the day of your trial?"

"Yes, sir, I do. Wanna see it? My Aunt Lucy kept it for me 'long with a few other personal belongings all these years. She brought it by yesterday with a pan of cornbread. I'll fetch it."

After a few minutes, Otis returned with a lantern and an old cigar box. Nick pulled his chair closer to the black man in order to get a good look at its contents. There was something reverent in the manner in which Otis opened the box. The lantern's light fell on the gold links of the bracelet and gentle hands handed it to Nick. It was polished to perfection, and as Nick examined each link, there was no sign of a medic alert symbol. Nor were there threads of yarn caught in the links.

"Where'd you get this?"

"Mama. She loved gold. When Owen got sick with diabetes, he had to wear a bracelet with one of those I.D. symbols in case he went into a coma. Mama was always fair with her twin sons. What one got, the other did, too. 'Cept mine never had no symbol. I guess I lucked out."

Nick's mind was racing. *Did Mike at the marina not say that a black man wearing a gold medic alert bracelet rented a kayak? Is there a connection?*

"Do you have a picture of you and Owen?"

Otis shook his head. "While I was in prison, there was a fire." This time the light from the lantern caught glistening tears drop from his cheeks into the box. "Mama never survived the smoke. Everything in the house burned. Nothing left."

Nick placed a comforting hand on his friend's shoulder. "I'm sorry." A moment of silence passed as Otis wiped away the wetness. "What else do you have in here?"

Nick watched as long black fingers picked up a photo of a beautiful ebony-skinned woman with an alluring smile. His forefinger traced the outline of her facial features and followed a mass of corkscrew ringlets that hung from the crown of her head.

"Corina." The name slipped from Otis's lips like soft velvet.

"Your sweetheart?"

"Fiance."

"What happened?"

This time his thick lips quivered and Otis could not speak. Instead, he handed Nick a letter and motioned for him to read it. The first line brought a tear to Nick's eye.

Dear Otis,
I won't be wearing your ring any longer…

Nick read the contents, folded it, then placed it back into the box before commenting, "Sometimes it helps to dump your bucket. Want to talk about it?"

"You're the first person to read that letter. Nobody know how it hurt the day I got it. Two years after I first went behind bars. Still hurts. I dream about her smooth chocolate skin and those eyes." Otis took a deep breath and continued, "All hope died that day, but to be honest, I couldn't blame her for breaking our engagement. No woman wants to wait eighteen years for a man."

For a moment, Nick's thoughts turned to Maureen. *Is it possible I can be losing her?*

"Did she marry?"

"Oh, yeah. Someone else married my Corina and promised to love her 'til death do them part. Another man planted the seeds of conception and she bore the children we planned to have. She live in Alabama now. Least that what my kinfolk tell me. Broken promises and memories is what I got outta the deal. I know I ain't the first man to have his heart broken, but it will always hurt. How 'bout you, Nick? You got a woman?"

A shadow crossed Nick's face. "I thought I did…up until a few days ago. She's not answering my calls and is acting kind of strange."

"Another man?"

"Might be. Thought she'd at least tell me. We met at work. She's a medical examiner, and so far things have been going great—lots in common, that sort of thing."

For the first time this evening, Otis gave Nick his best smile. "Her loss, if you ask me. Hey, where you want to lay out that sleepin' bag? Inside or out?'

"How about right here on the porch. It's been a while since I woke up with the sun. Goodnight. Remember, tomorrow is a new beginning."

Chapter Nineteen

By eight-forty-five a.m., Nick and Otis pulled into the courthouse parking lot and took one of the visitor spaces. Otis spoke little on the drive into town. Nick suspected old memories of this building lay heavy on his mind. After clearing security at the door, they walked down the hallway to Judge Allen's chamber.

Halfway there, an office door marked State Attorney flung open and out stepped Samuel Wilson. He stopped, nodded to Nick, then for a brief moment stared at Otis.

The look in Sam's eyes and the sudden stiffening of Otis's body indicated to Nick that the two recognized each other, though not a word passed between them.

"Let it go, Otis," advised Nick as they walked on."This is no time or place to make a scene."

"You're right. Just haunted by old memories, that's all."

A few yards down the hall, a gold-plated nameplate on a door spelled out the name Judge William Allen. Before entering, Nick turned to Otis. "Take a deep breath, say a prayer, or whatever it takes to look calm."

Nick patted his companion on the back and gave him an encouraging smile. "Remember, I'm on your side."

Once inside, the secretary led them to the proper chamber. Judge Allen offered his hand in greeting, then got right to the point of the meeting.

"Gentlemen, before I give you my decision, I'd like to hear firsthand Mr. Washington's recollection of his actions the night Judge Ramsey was murdered." He looked at Otis and nodded. "Go ahead."

At first, Otis's voice was weak and nervous, but as he retraced his steps, he regained his confidence and a steady flow of words came out of his mouth. His eyes never wavered from the judge and he held his head high.

"And that's the truth, your Honor."

A short silence filled the room with expectation until the judge turned to Nick and questioned him.

"You're acting as a character witness?"

"Yes, sir. I've known this man since I was a young lad."

Judge Allen turned his attention to Otis. "You're a lucky man. Because I know Lieutenant Melino. He's an honest man, and I'm impressed that he's willing to put his reputation on the line for you. I'm putting you under house arrest, Mr. Washington. You'll wear a GPS ankle bracelet until it can be proven you are innocent. Should you remove the device for any reason you'll find yourself behind bars. Is that understood?"

"Yes, sir."

The judge buzzed his secretary and asked her to tell a deputy to bring a tracking device to his office. With that done, Nick and Otis shook Judge Allen's hand and made a retreat to the car.

Relief eased the taut look across Otis's brow and he sat back in his seat and closed his eyes. As they drove back toward Blackwater Bay, he made a surprising statement.

"I gotta tell you something', Nick. Deep down in my gut I know Owen the one who drove that hijacked car. He got himself mixed up with that low life cousin of ours and they run with a wild crowd. Used to brag about how many vehicles they steal in one weekend. Don't understand how he keeps himself out of prison."

"So he's one step ahead of the law. Is that what you're telling me?"

"He gots somethin' goin' for him, that's for sure."

Nick looked over at Otis. "If it will make you feel better, chew on this a while. His kind always slip up eventually. The law will catch up with him."

As the sign 'Blackwater Marina' came into view, something from the marina triggered a sudden revelation in Nick's mind. *Why haven't I thought of this 'til now?* Anxious to explore it further, he said to his passenger, "Otis when we get to the camp I need you to take a paddle and slap me up one side of the head and down the other."

Two black eyes widened and looked at Nick in disbelief. "What? You gone crazy? I's in enough trouble. Sure don't need to be beatin' on some policeman!" Otis noticed the grin on Nick's face. "You teasin', right?"

"I've had my mind on so many things these past couple days, this never occurred to me. Listen. When you were fishing in the bay around the bend from where the party barge was anchored, did you hear an outboard motor at all?"

Otis took his time to answer. "No, I didn't. Not before the shots or after. It was quiet. Just the croak of some bullfrogs and the hoot of an owl in the distance."

"Don't you think that's kind of strange? You'd think the murderer would want to high tail it out of that area in the fastest way he could."

"Yeah. Like in one of those speedboats that stir up this bay. Seems like he would. Whatcha got on your mind?"

"Kayak. It was almost dark and a good kayaker could maneuver around by making little to no noise. Bang! Bang! He shoots his target and silently paddles away into the shadows."

"Oh, man, Lieutenant, that gonna be hard to track down. No registration numbers to trace. Lots of folks got them things nowadays."

"I didn't say it'd be easy, but you're here on the water. Keep an eye out for a lime green one with the Blackwater logo on the side. The guys over at the marina lost one this week."

As Nick drove back to work, Mike's words formed a picture in his thoughts*: marina, missing kayak, black dude, gold medic alert bracelet, rental form alias. Could Owen Washington finally have made his biggest mistake?*

Chapter Twenty

Rodney Santia began his day in a bad mood. The news from his office in Boston ignited a flame in his ulcer. He hadn't expected Worldwide Investments to be targeted by the Security and Exchange Commission for the third time. *My tracks should be covered by now. The cost of paying the 'big boys' behind the scenes to turn their heads is getting expensive.*

Rod looked out the oversized window in his country bungalow. Scattered along Blackwater Bay, homes demolished by Hurricane Ivan, were now being rebuilt up on pilings. In front of Judge Ramsey's home, a flag representing the state of Florida flew at half-mast. As the wind furled and unfurled its fabric, the pain in Rod's stomach intensified.

Since coming to the Panhandle for his annual spring break, things had not gone as planned. Yesterday's luncheon with Maureen was a disaster. Rod lit a marijuana joint and inhaled deeply.

She thought she could run, but I showed her she can't hide. A smirk teased the edges of his thin lips. *Wasn't hard to find her, either. My private P.I. convinced all the right people to talk. She'll see things my way. A little physical persuasion always brings her type around. Right now, I've got a few words for my buddy, Sam.* Rod's smirk turned into an evil grin. *Doesn't hurt to have a State Attorney friend with his hand out. He'll earn his compensation this time or the Santia 'family association' will pay him a visit.*

Rod dialed Sam's cell number, took a long drag on the joint, and blew smoke across the room. By the third ring, he was ready to hang up, but the fourth attempt brought a response.

A familiar voice answered, "Sam speaking."

"So are you at home or work?"

"Work. I've got a trial in two hours and I stepped out for a coffee. You're up early for a man on vacation."

"Wouldn't be if it weren't for that secretary of mine. Can't seem to get it through her head that Central Time means when I'm in northwest Florida, I'm an hour behind Boston time. Oh well, she has other attributes." The two men enjoyed a chuckle. Rod's tone changed as he continued, "She woke me up with bad news—affects you, too."

"What is it?"

"The SEC is on my tail again. Could be they're following up on that letter you told me Ramsey sent to them."

"So what's new? They've had letters of complaint before and nothing's come of their so-called investigation. Nothing to worry about. You know how to handle it."

"It's different this time. It came from a judge. A higher authority than some Joe off the street. They'll take this one seriously. We need to act fast. Get that file Ramsey showed you and we'll shred it here at the house. I've already instructed my office assistant in Boston to dispose of any evidence that Worldwide Investments ever did business with the man."

"Whoa. Things don't work that fast down here. This courthouse is crawling with security. I need time to work out a plan. I can see the headlines tomorrow—'State Attorney arrested for Break-in.'"

"Get that dealer to do the job. It's probably all in a day's work for him."

"Owen?"

"Yeah. I can't complain about what he did for me. Sam, if I go down, you go with me and there goes that lifetime chance to sit on the bench. They'll be making an appointment to replace Ramsey soon, won't they?"

"That's just the tip of my iceberg, pal."

Rod finished the joint and asked, "What do you mean? You in some hot water?"

Sam hesitated then confessed, "Something's come out of the past that could get me disbarred."

A mocking gasp erupted from Rod. "You! Squeaky clean, Samuel Wilson? Upstanding community servant! No way!"

"Have your fun, Rod, but I'm serious. In my race to the top, I withheld evidence that would have cleared a man. Instead, an innocent man went to prison for eighteen years. The victim is starting to remember the night of the incident and her story has changed. Judge Ramsey, the defense attorney and I had a meeting not too long ago. The judge told us he intended to examine the situation and it was possible a new trial was in order."

"But the judge is dead, so that's the end of that."

Rod heard the fear in his friend's voice.

"Not if Robert Swift has his way. Another judge will take over. If the truth comes out, my career in law is over."

"Sounds as though you might be between a rock and a hard place. If the state finds out you've been taking a cut from every customer you've sent to Worldwide as well as working as a State Attorney, you're going to be looking out from behind those bars, partner."

"Okay, I'll get with Owen and see what we can work out? Anything else on your mind? You've certainly been a ray of sunshine this morning."

"As a matter of fact, there is. You know most of the people in this town, right?"

The pride in Sam's response was obvious. "Well…anyone who has any influence. Why?"

"Tell me about Nick Melino."

"Aha, the Sheriff's Office head detective. From what I've seen in court when he's been called as a witness, he's cool, smart, and won't give up until he gets his man or woman as the case may be. And…" Sam chose his words carefully, "he dates Maureen."

"Not for long as far as I'm concerned. I'm taking her back north with me—one way or another. I've spent a bunch of money tracking her down since she skipped town almost two years ago. She's the kind of woman a man dreams about. Melino can go fish somewhere else. This one belongs to me."

Sam laughed. "Don't be too sure of yourself. Have you never heard that love is a lot like fishing? The best one always gets away."

"Get back to work, Sam. You may not be working for the state much longer." Before Sam could respond, a faint beep in his ear ended the conversation.

Chapter Twenty-One

The text message Sam sent Owen read: "Urgent. Meet at my beach house after dark."

* * *

"You want me to do what? You crazy, man. This courthouse not some dinky shop. Alarms go off. Police come runnin'. No way!"

"Calm down. You can bypass security. I've got a key to the side door I often use when I'm working on a case after hours. One of those window cutters should take care of the glass in the secretary's door. You'll have to go through her office to get to the judge's chamber. Dress down and wear a cap. Strap one of the custodian vacuum cleaners over your shoulder. They keep them in the storage room. It'll be open."

"Sounds risky to me. What you want from the judge's chamber you can't ask his secretary to get?"

"That's none of her business. I want a file folder with the name Worldwide Investments on it." Sam handed Owen a piece of paper with the words written in black ink. "Go through every drawer in his desk and file cabinet. Wear gloves. Leave no prints behind."

"That gonna take time. The longer I stay in there the greater the risk."

"What's the matter? You losing your nerve. Used to be you bragged about this sort of thing."

Owen scratched his head and pondered the situation.

"Ten thousand and not a penny less."

Sam sealed the deal with a handshake. "You bring the file and I'll bring the money."

"When you want the job done?"

"Tonight."

* * *

Darkness intensified the gloom Maureen felt for the last three days. Since seeing Rod in David's Catfish House, she feared for her safety. *My past has caught up with me*, she sighed. *Just when I thought that brutal man was out of my life.*

Her eyes scanned the forensic parking area for any suspicious vehicles hidden in the shadows. Satisfied she was alone, she pressed her car's key fob and ran to open the door. After locking herself in, Maureen's aching head dropped into trembling hands and her tired eyes closed.

My life's turning into a nightmare. I can't think straight and it's beginning to affect my work. How could I have forgotten to take Nick the prints? I tagged the wrong corpse this morning, and even Andy looked at me puzzled when I snapped at him for dropping a scalpel. At this rate, I'll be out of a job.

Call Nick, her inner voice begged, but every time Maureen reached for her phone and began to press the numbers, she stopped at the last digit. *He doesn't deserve the cold shoulder treatment. Ignoring his calls. But I refuse to get him involved in this mess. I need to get away. Houston is advertising for a medical examiner. I need to call them.*

Every few seconds Maureen looked in her rear view mirror to be sure she wasn't being followed. Finally, her street sign appeared and in no time, she maneuvered her car into its usual parking spot. Once again, she looked around but saw no one. As she jogged up the porch steps, a voice she dreaded stopped her cold and a slender man stepped out of the darkness and blocked her way.

"Late getting home from work, aren't you?"

Maureen felt as though her heart was going to beat itself to death. A sickening weakness threatened to buckle her legs and her mouth went dry. She turned to run but he was too fast for her and grabbed her wrist twisting it until she winced.

"Leave me alone. I told you we're finished. I want nothing more to do with you. Yes, I know your little secret, but I've told no one. Believe me, Rod."

"I think you remember the men in my family don't take no for answer." His grip tightened. "You're coming back to Boston with me one way or another. And don't think your cop boyfriend can stop me. Melino, right? I checked him out. Frequents the restaurant you two were at the other night."

A surprised gasp brought additional fear to Maureen and she knew struggling against this man was wasted effort.

"Let go of me! Help!" She screamed. Instantly, the back of Rod's hand met the softness of her cheek and the sting of his assault brought tears to her eyes.

"That's just for starters, honey. You'll see things my way." With that, he jerked her to the ground and disappeared into the night.

Maureen lay at the foot of the steps dazed and petrified. The sound of an opening door soon brought an elderly neighbor. He recognized her at once and hurried to her side.

"Maureen, what happened? I thought I heard a scream. Here, let me help you up. How did you fall?"

Shaken, Maureen's mind spun a tale. *I can't tell him the truth.*

"Oh, it's my own fault, Murray. I worked late and the porch light isn't on. I guess I tripped on a step. Nothing serious. I'll be fine."

"Well, are you sure? I can call 911."

Her response was quick and direct. "No! No! Please just let me take your hand to steady myself. Thank you for your concern."

Safely inside her condo, Maureen bolted the door and checked every window. Common sense should have told her to call Nick, or at least the authorities, but fear won the battle. Instead, she hobbled to the bathroom and examined her wounds in the mirror. Her cheek, still red, bore signs of a bruise and the bones in her wrist throbbed. A scratch on her leg where she hit the cement sidewalk oozed blood.

A hot shower will help, she thought. *At least nothing is broken—this time.* I've got to get away from him. Soon.

A sleeping pill finally eased the tormenting thoughts that battered her anxious mind. For a few hours, she felt safe.

Chapter Twenty-Two

The constant ringing of Nick's office phone jangled his morning nerves and he fumbled with his keys, spilling his sacred java on his polished shoes.

"Okay already. Give a man a chance to get in."

He threw his keys on the desk and picked up the receiver. "Lieutenant Melino."

"Lieutenant, this is Mary Murphy. Something terrible has happened." Mary's words tumbled out of her mouth with rapidity."

"Slow down, Mary, and take a deep breath." Nick waited until the woman got herself in control. "Now, where are you and what happened?"

"I'm at the courthouse. In my office. I called 911 first, but then I thought you were the one who needed to know."

"Tell me, Mary."

"When I came to work this morning, the glass in my door was shattered and bits and pieces scattered all over the floor. In fact, the door was open. I called security and they came running to check things out. Nothing in my area was touched or stolen, but Judge Ramsey's door had been tampered with and left open as well. Whoever was here was in a hurry looking for something because all the desk drawers and file cabinets were wide open. Not one was back in its place. The strange part is I can't see anything of value missing."

"Mary, listen. Has anyone besides Connor and me been in that room since we last were there? It's important, so think hard. One of his peers? Family, maybe?"

"No, the family told me they'd be in to clean out his chamber next week. I'm positive you and your partner are the only ones."

"Don't let anyone get past your desk. I'm on my way. Thanks for the call, Mary."

Nick looked at his coffee growing cold and decided it was a lost cause. He was past the front reception desk when Connor walked in.

"Turn around. We're on our way to the courthouse. There's been a break in last night."

"Good morning to you, too." Connor scoffed then asked, "What's going on?"

"Judge Ramsey's chamber was ransacked."

"Where was security?"

"Beats me. Probably watching basketball. March Madness time."

The detectives made their way through several police officers and the usual curious onlookers.

"It's all yours, Lieutenant," offered one of the security men. "Just as we found it."

A mass of paperwork covered the floor, but everything else looked as it had a week ago.

"Connor, call the lab and have them send someone down to check for prints. My guess is the culprit wore gloves, but we need to be sure. I'm going to check out the desk."

The same mess spilled out over most of the desk drawers, but the top of the desk held only a lamp, a phone and a gold-plated pen holder with "Judge Ramsey" inscribed on the surface. "Wait a minute," thought Nick aloud. *There is something missing. The financial folder with Worldwide Investments written across the front.*

Nick looked at Connor and waited until he was finished with his call. "Remember, we looked at a financial statement and I told you even though it was the judge's personal information, I felt it was part of the investigation. I put it back where I found it." Nick tapped his finger on the exact spot. "It's gone, and Mary told me no one else has been in here since that day."

"Maybe Mary placed it somewhere. Let me ask her." Connor walked back to her office but returned with a negative report. "She insists that she's not touched one item."

"Someone wants that file in a big way. I'm hoping Glenda has a copy. I'll give her a call. I want to take another look at it. Looks as though it's shaping up for a busy day, partner. And I didn't even get my coffee yet."

Chapter Twenty-Three

With Glenda Ramsey's permission, Nick brought Calvin Tooley, a financial advisor, to the meeting. After the initial introductions, Nick explained, "As you know, this is not my field, Glenda, so I've asked my trusted friend to help us interpret these statements from Worldwide Investments. He works with one of our local banks and knows more about investing than I could ever imagine."

Glenda gave Mr. Tolley a smile of confidence and put her hand on Nick's arm.

"Come, gentlemen, we'll sit at the dining room table. It's wide enough to spread out the paperwork and no one will be cramped."

Displayed on a large oval oak table were files organized by years. Calvin adjusted his black-rimmed glasses and extracted a calculator, a pen, and a pad of plain paper from his briefcase. Before Glenda sat, he asked her, "How long have you dealt with Worldwide Investments?"

"Five years."

"How did you hear of them? Frankly, I've never run across that company."

"Samuel Wilson, the State Attorney, advised my husband to get in on the ground floor. He even showed Henry his statements."

Tolley's eyebrows raised a notch at this news, but he kept silent and let Glenda continue.

"They were certainly more than our CDs at the bank offered." Glenda's face flushed and she stammered, "Oh, forgive me. I didn't mean to be critical, but they were tempting."

"No offense, taken ma'am. The financial world is a competitive field." Tolley reached for the first file.

Nick and Glenda recognized his need for space so they moved to the end of the table and conversed in hushed tones.

"Lieutenant, I was shocked this morning to hear of the break-in. Sarah and I need to go down there and clean out Henry's personal things." A cloud of sadness swept across her porcelain face. "It's not a task I relish. So many memories, you know."

Nick patted her hand. "Sometimes, I'm told, it's best to get it over with."

"You may be right. But why would someone want our personal finance information?"

"That's why I've engaged Calvin's expertise. There may be a clue in the numbers."

Before he continued his exchange of ideas, Nick felt the vibration of his cell phone in his jacket pocket.

"Excuse me, I don't want to distract Calvin so I'll step outside and take this."

Once on the patio, he answered, "Lieutenant Melino."

"Nick, it's Andy." An unfamiliar subdued tone didn't square with Andy's usual greeting. "Can you talk?"

Puzzled, Nick replied. “I’m at the Ramsey residence. There’s an issue that’s come up which may have a bearing on the case.”

Again, Andy’s voice sounded strange. “Call my cell as soon as you’re free. It’s urgent.”

Before Nick could respond, a beep ended the conversation.

That’s not like Andy. I wonder if he wants to talk about the case? Maybe forensics has found something they missed at the autopsy.

Another thought caused him to start pressing Andy’s number on his cell’s pad. *Maureen. Was he trying to tell him something about Maureen?*

As his phone started to ring, Glenda called from the doorway, “Nick, Mr. Tolley needs to talk to you.” Frustrated by the interruption, Nick’s fingers cut off the phone’s connection. However, he put on his best face and walked back into the dining room.

“There’s something that bothers me about these statements, Nick. With the shape our economy has been in these past few years, returns on all investments have fluctuated considerably. But Worldwide has consistently paid out an above average percentage, particularly the first few years the Ramsey’s were involved. Now that the economy is showing improvement and most companies are posting gains, suddenly it doesn’t make sense that loses appear. Something is not right.”

Glenda cut in, “That’s what bothered Henry. In fact he had a meeting with Samuel and asked him to explain the significant difference. He thought Samuel could shed some light on it, but according to Henry, the State Attorney got upset, especially when Henry told him he was going to send a letter to the SEC that night.”

Calvin removed his glasses and wiped his brow. "Mrs. Ramsey, I hate to tell you this, but I have a suspicion that you've been scammed."

Before she could respond, Nick eyes widened and he blurted out, "Ponzi scheme! Is that where you're going with this, Calvin?"

The man nodded and replied, "Afraid so."

"Ponzi scheme? Gentlemen, you've lost me? Please explain."

Nick looked at his friend. "You tell her. I'm sure to confuse things worse than they are."

Glenda's brow's knit together in worry. "Please, Mr. Tolley, I'm not familiar with the term. By the look on both your faces, it doesn't sound good."

Calvin took a deep breath and prepared to explain it as simply as he could.

"Ma'am, these frauds are normally started by one man, a master mind who takes your money and talks a big game. Tells you you'll get huge returns on your investments. And you do the first few years because he doesn't invest your money at all. He uses money you gave him and lets on its returns from the initial investments. He is always shuffling money from one party to another. First he takes a slice off the top for himself, then he uses the rest to pay off the first group of investors." Calvin stopped to be sure Glenda understood.

"Sort of like robbing Peter to pay Paul like that Madof character in New York did?"

Calvin chuckled, "Sort of, ma'am. In order for his clients to believe his company is on the up and up, he actually does invest some of his money in blue chip companies. Not yours. The Ponzi hustler has to be continually bringing in new investors to pay each level their returns. And here is where I believe Judge Ramsey got suspicious. As the cycle continues, it gets more and more complicated and earlier levels of investors will get antsy if they don't continue to see favorable returns. My guess is that this hustler is running out of new blood since the past couple years folks have held onto their money for fear of a collapse."

"Dear Lord," Glenda's voice was a whisper. "What am I to do?"

"Well, I can tell you I'll be making a few calls to the SEC in Boston tomorrow for a start," Nick offered. "At this point it's conjecture, Glenda, but we'll see if the government boys can shake Worldwide Investment's tree. One never knows what will come out of it."

"Sounds like a plan to me, Nick." Tolley grinned before he continued, "You're pretty good at ruffling feathers."

* * *

By the time Nick left the Ramsey residence and turned onto Highway 90 towards Milton, his phone made connection with Andy's. He knew driving and talking on a cell phone wasn't encouraged by the sheriff, but his curiosity invoked by Andy's earlier call needed to be satisfied.

"Hey, Andy. Nick here. What's up? I'm in my car so we can talk now."

Again, Nick strained to hear Andy's voice.

"It's Maureen. Something is going on with her. She's not herself."

"What'd you mean?"

"She came in this morning wearing an ace bandage on her wrist and I swear her makeup tried to cover up a bruise. I've been around battered bodies long enough to recognize a bruise when I see it. When I asked her what happened she told me she fell going up her porch steps."

"You don't believe her?"

"I might have if that man who took her out to lunch a few days ago hadn't showed up again. Maureen went white when she saw him at the door."

"Give me a description of the guy, Andy."

"Of course I wasn't staring at him. Actually, I was cleaning up the floor after an autopsy, but I did take a few glimpses."

"So, what did he look like?" Nick's anxiety grew.

"Tall. Sort of like one of those Mediterranean type guys—olive complexion, dark hair."

"Did you hear their conversation?"

"Only bits and pieces. I heard enough to realize Maureen was in no mood to deal with him. Told him 'no' several times and finally asked him to leave. His last words were 'Later, baby.' She slammed the door in his face. She's got guts, I'll tell you that."

"She gave you no explanation of who he is or why he keeps showing up?"

"Nup. None. Went back to her office and closed the door. She hasn't come out since. It's almost quitting time and I see no move to leave. I think she's scared to go home, Nick. Just a feelin' I got."

Nick's foot pressed down on the accelerator and the car sped forward. "Andy, I'm on my way to the morgue. Please don't let her out of your sight. And one more thing. Don't mention my name."

"Gotcha."

Chapter Twenty-Four

Different scenarios flashed through Nick's mind and it was difficult to keep his attention on his driving. *Why is this man showing up at Maureen's work unexpectedly? Is she afraid of him? I want some answers. Today.* Determination replaced the baffled look he wore earlier.

As Nick parked his Camaro near the building, he scanned the lot for a man fitting the description Andy gave him. No suspicious characters sat in vehicles or stood anywhere in sight, so he walked to his destination.

Andy met him at the door.

"She hasn't left yet. Second office on the right. I'm out of here. Got a ball game tonight. Maureen can lock up."

Nick held out his hand to offer his thanks. "I appreciate the tip, friend. I'll try to get to the bottom of this."

Andy smiled and gave Nick a pat on his shoulder. "That's why you're the detective."

Even though Nick knew the autopsy room looked clean, a faint odor of chemicals lingered in the air. His stomach lurched. *Never could stand the smell of this place.* The click of his heels on the tile floor echoed through the eerie silence, and in Nick's mind, death permeated the whole environment.

When he saw the name plate, "Maureen O'Shanesy Medical Examiner," on the office door, he stopped, softly knocked, and in a gentle voice announced himself.

"Maureen, it's Nick."

No response.

"We need to talk. I know you're in there. Please open the door."

Every nerve in his body sent the adrenaline rushing from his head to his toe. *Waiting is not my forte, honey. Thirty more seconds and I'm coming in."*

As he reached for the doorknob, a small crack of light gradually enlarged until an open door revealed a weeping woman. Maureen took one look at the man standing before her and all of her resistance dissolved. They reached for each other until two bodies melded into one.

Through a torrent of tears, she cried, "I'm so sorry. If I've hurt you, please forgive me. I wanted to answer your calls, but I have no right to draw you into this mess I've created."

Nick felt her wince as her cheek pressed against his face.

"What mess? Your life seemed perfectly fine to me."

"My past life, Nick. There are things I haven't told you."

Nick pulled far enough away to look into her swollen eyes. "Then it's time you did, don't you think? I didn't fall in love with you to be put on the back burner. Fess up, girl." A tender smile gave Maureen the courage to continue her story.

As she led Nick to the divan behind her desk, she pulled a stack of tissues from a box.

"I'll need these," she said. "It's not a pretty picture. Andy told you I've had a visitor, didn't he?"

Nick nodded. "I can't wait to hear who he is."

Maureen took a breath and swiped the wetness as well as a portion of her makeup from her face. Bluish-black skin on her upper cheekbone revealed the nasty-looking shiner.

Nick squeezed her shaking hand and she gained her composure.

"His name is Rodney Santia. He lives in Boston. His family has connections in the underworld."

Nick couldn't contain himself. "The Mafia? How in the world did you meet someone like that?"

"He sought me out. The truth is he watches the obituary page in the newspapers and then uses the computer to gain personal information. A month after the death of my husband, I got a call from him expressing his sympathy. He told me he knew Adam from the business world. I had no reason not to believe him because Adam was a bank manager. I thought that was the end of it, but a couple weeks later he called again and asked me to have lunch with him. He said he had something important to show me. I agreed."

Maureen sniffed and wiped her nose.

"Go on," urged Nick.

"I told you when we first started going to AA that after I lost my child and husband in the auto accident, I used alcohol to numb the pain. I wasn't thinking straight. I should never have accepted his invitation. Oh, Rod was very gracious, understanding, and suave at the beginning. He even talked me into investing ten thousand dollars from my insurance money with his company—Worldwide Investments."

Nick almost came off the couch. "Did you say Worldwide Investments?"

Startled, Maureen came back, "Yes. You've heard of them?"

"Not until recently. Judge Ramsey was involved with that company, too. But let me hear your tale first and then I'll fill you in on what I learned today."

"As the months rolled on, Rod's calls became frequent and we spent more time together. Dinners, theatre, kayaking, outings with his family. He even took me flying in his private plane. I guess one might say we were dating. I felt guilty since I was a recent widow, but he assured me I was doing nothing wrong. After six months, he pressed for a deeper relationship." Maureen lowered her head and a pink blush crept up her neck and colored her cheeks. "You know, a physical one."

Nick nodded. "That doesn't surprise me."

"I held him off, but I sensed agitation every time he didn't get his way. When we attended functions he was very possessive of me and jealous of any male attention I received." New tears puddled in Maureen's eyes. "One night he struck me. Told me I belonged to him. Another time he flew into a rage and broke my little finger. The more he showed his true self, the more I drank to hide my fear."

This time, Nick took a tissue and dabbed the liquid from Maureen's face.

"If it hadn't been for Adam's financial knowledge, I would never have become suspicious of the returns I received on my Worldwide investments. We often discussed different ways to make profit on our income. One of them sounded very familiar to what Rod was doing. But Adam explained it was made up of fraudulent investing. One of those 'too good to be true' ventures."

"Then why did you do it?"

"Like I told you, he's slick and I was vulnerable. One of the telltale signs that made me suspect something was not Kosher was Rod's insistence I recruit my friends to invest with him, too. Some did, to my shame."

"You could have taken your suspicions to the Securities Commission. Why didn't you?"

"Fear. By this time in our relationship, I did do a little research into his background and found out the SEC had investigated Worldwide but found nothing illegal. I dropped the whole issue and decided it best if I got as far away from Boston as I could. North West Florida seemed to be the spot, but I guess I was wrong. I spent the afternoon rewriting my resume. There's an opening in Houston."

Nick's response was quick. "No. No more running. I'm going to bring this lowlife in on assault charges."

This time it was Maureen who protested. Please, Nick, I'm okay. Let it lie. It won't do any good. He has connections that do his bidding. They'll hurt you. I've seen and heard how they operate. Besides, that kind of charge won't put him away for good. We need the SEC to do their job and bring Rod down."

Nick took Maureen's hand again. Her eyes begged him to listen to her. He relented, but it came with a qualifier.

"I've got to get you to a safe place. He's probably watching my house, so you can't go there. And you are definitely not returning to your condo. That's a no-brainer."

"But where will I go?"

Nick saw desperation cloud her face and for a second he had no answer. Then it came to him—the fish camp. Perfect—out of town, isolated, with someone to keep watch.

Nick jumped up and pulled her with him. "Grab your things, sweetheart, I've got you a new residence. Now, I have to warn you, there are few amenities, but you'll love the view. Grab your things we're on our way."

"Where, Nick, where?"

"To meet Otis Washington."

Maureen knew there was no point in arguing, but as Nick opened the passenger side door, she exclaimed, "Wait! My car. I can't leave it here."

"I'll have a patrol car bring someone to get it. Get your keys ready."

In less than five minutes, a deputy pulled up and Nick instructed one of the officers to follow him in the white Nissan.

As reality sank in, Maureen's mind was in a whirl. "Nick, I need to get clothes, toiletries, you know—women's stuff."

Nick reached into his jacket and pulled out his cell phone. He winked at her and smiled as he connected with a number. After the second ring, Maureen heard the one-sided conversation.

"Sis, I've got a favor to ask." A second went by as he listened then began. "This is going to sound a little weird, but hear me out. I need you to go to Walmart or one of those stores where you women shop and pick up a few things for a friend of mine. Now get a pencil to make a list."

Again, there was a pause in Nick's speech as he waited for his sister Peggy to find some paper. "Okay, ready? She'll need shirts, a pair of jeans, shorts, some sandals and of course…under garments."

Maureen's look of astonishment coincided with her protest. "What are you doing? I can't let you…"

She didn't get a chance to finish. Peggy's next question teetered on the personal side.

"Sizes?"

Nick, coyly surveyed his passenger from head to foot then said, "I'm going to need your input here. Let's start from the bottom and work to the top. Sandals?"

Maureen hesitated then complied, "Six and a half."

"Jeans?"

"Twelve."

"Shirt?"

"Ten."

A flush of pink lit up Nick's cheeks and he lowered his voice. "I…" he paused before continuing, "don't think I'll ask that one. About Penny's size, okay?"

"Thanks, sis, I'll be around to get them in a couple hours. Oh, she'll need a toothbrush and soap, too. Love, ya. Bye."

Chapter Twenty-Five

Otis looked up from mending his mullet net when he heard two cars turning into his driveway. He identified Nick's Camaro, but the second was unknown to him. Without hesitation, he put aside his project and walked toward his visitors.

Nick worked his way out from behind the wheel and soon a good looking woman with shining red hair hovered close to him.

"Hey there," greeted Nick, "how's it going?"

"Doin' fine. Just fixin' a hole in my fish net. Darn things are getting' old." Otis chuckled, "Can't catch nothin' if them mullet swim right through it."

Otis glanced at Maureen with male approval and extended his hand in greeting. "Otis Washington, ma'am. Welcome."

Maureen responded with her best smile, but before she spoke, Nick cut in. "This is Maureen O'Shanesy. We need your help, friend."

"Anything. I owe you, man. What can I do?"

Nick got right to the point and explained the need to shelter Maureen. By the time he finished, the expression on Otis's face turned from puzzlement to concern.

"Ain't much, ma'am, but you sure enough welcome."

"Thank you." Maureen's words of appreciation came from her heart as relief washed over her stressed body and a tightness around her lips disappeared.

"C'mon, make yourself comfortable." He pointed to a couple of wooden lawn chairs on the porch. From the look of the peeling paint, they'd seen better days.

Anxious to complete his errands, Nick declined the offer and turned to Maureen. "I'm going back to town to pick up the things you need. I'll be a couple of hours, okay? Besides, I gotta get the deputy back on his turf." Nick chuckled. "Don't need the sheriff down my neck for abusing privileges. Do you have your cell?"

Maureen fumbled around in her purse until she felt its familiar shape.

"Right here. I charged it earlier today."

"Keep it close and if you need me or remembered something I forgot, call."

Otis winked at Maureen and teased, "Get outta here, Lieutenant. Miz Maureen and me gots some serious getting' acquaintin' to do."

Nick leaned down and planted a soft kiss on Maureen's forehead. "Take care of my gal, Otis. I'm counting on you."

* * *

For the next four days, Nick spent his evenings at the fish camp. It was pure joy to see the change in Maureen. Her lilting laughter brought a relaxed smile to her tanned cheeks and sunburned nose. She appeared to feel comfortable in the humble home and the interaction between her and Otis spoke of a growing bond of friendship.

Of course, another incentive for Nick's frequent visitations was the delicious meal set before him each night.

"Otis is teaching me to make collard and mustard greens," boasted Maureen. "The secret is in the smoked ham hocks. Boil them until the meat falls off the bone then throw them in the pot with salt and pepper." Another mouthful crossed her pink lips.

Nick dug his fork into the greens and teased, "You sure you don't have a streak of southern blood running through your veins?"

Otis joined the conversation. "Irish, she tells me. Here, try a piece of this here Irish Soda bread." He passed the plate to Nick. "Every bit as good as my cornbread. And I'm gonna brag on her some more. She gigged the biggest flounder we caught last night. You getting' the hang of it, Miz. Maureen."

Maureen took the compliment in stride. "Has to be my teacher. He knows what he's doing."

Nick chimed in with, "You know what I think?" The questioning expression he received from both his dinner companions encouraged him to continue. "You, my dear, are having entirely too much fun down here."

Maureen playfully nudged him with her leg under the table.

"No argument from me."

"Well, considering I convinced your boss to put you on vacation, I guess you're entitled."

Surprise beamed on Maureen's face and she put her utensils on her plate.

"You talked to Dr. Mainer? He knows the circumstances?"

"Enough to do his best to protect you. He doesn't want to lose you either."

Maureen reached over and kissed Nick's cheek.

Otis, sensing that three was a crowd, cleared his throat and gave an order. "Okay you two, I want you out of my kitchen. Scram!"

Neither Nick nor Maureen put up an argument and headed for the front door. They strolled along the bay's edge and listened to the evening songs of the birds as they readied themselves for the night. Neither spoke, but with arms entwined around each other's waist they walked in perfect bliss and harmony.

As the sun made its final bow from the horizon, Nick spotted a beached log and suggested they sit for awhile. Settled into the crook of Nick's arm, Maureen grew serious.

"Forgive me for breaking this idyllic moment, but there are questions I want to ask you and we don't get the opportunity to have private conversations."

"Sure, I understand. What do you want to discuss?"

"Were you able to contact the SEC in Boston?"

"It took some doing, but I finally got to talk to the new director, a Mr. Kincaid." Nick sighed, "I have no patience with bureaucracy. It stinks. I have to admit, though, he was decent, especially when I told him Judge Ramsey was shot. I asked if his agency received a letter from Henry asking for an investigation and he assured me it was top priority."

"Well that's encouraging." Maureen patted Nick's arm.

"I asked about previous investigations into Worldwide's business practices and he told me something interesting."

Maureen sat up, all ears.

"The lead investigator disappeared two years ago. Not a trace of the man. The SEC isn't sure if Worldwide paid him off and he skipped the country or if he fell into harm's way."

"I vote for the latter. My guess is that he's at the bottom of Boston Harbor. That's the Santia style—get rid of the evidence."

"Unfortunately, the ball was dropped under the old director and nobody cared to pick it up—until now. They've called in the FBI."

"Why can't they come down here and arrest Rod for fraud.?"

"It has to be proven. The case against him must be ironclad in order to stand up in court and that takes time. Maureen," Nick spoke softly, "you realize you may be called as a character witness because of your close relationship with Rod and his family."

A shiver went through Maureen and she snuggled closer to Nick. "I never thought of that, but you're right." A moment of silence passed and she added, "But I'll do it if it means putting that scum behind bars for the rest of his life."

Nick squeezed her shoulder and teased, "That's my gal. They don't call you folks the Fighting Irish for nothing."

* * *

Owen fondled the money he held in his right hand. Ten one-thousand dollar bills. *Easy money. That break-in* was *a piece of cake.* As he recounted the wad, a new thought emerged. *Why not squeeze Samuel a little harder? Blackmail could be quite lucrative.*

He sat on the edge of the bed and put his head in his hands. *Think smart. Think smart.* After several minutes, he let out an audible cry of triumph.

"I've got it! Yes, this ought to keep me in the green for a long time."

A squirm rustled the sheets next to him and a female cooed, "Who you talkin' to, sweetie. What you got?"

"Nothin yet, but I goin' too."

With a flick of his wrist, he turned off the light. "Sweet dreams, baby."

Chapter Twenty-Six

"Lieutenant, wait up," called an officer at the reception desk.

Nick turned back toward the front doors. "Morning Lou. What's up?"

"A call came in about ten minutes ago for you. A fella named Alex from Blackwater Marina says it may be important."

"Oh, what is it?"

"Wouldn't tell me. Wants to talk to you. Here's his number." Lou passed Nick a Post-It note.

"Thanks, soon as I get my caffeine for the day I'll give him a shout."

Hmm, thought Nick, *maybe he's got something new to add to the Ramsey case. Think I'll skip the coffee."*

In short order, Nick settled into his office routine and dialed the number in hand.

"Blackwater Marina," a familiar voice answered.

"Lieutenant Melino, here. I'm returning your call. Something you need to tell me?"

"Morning, Lieutenant. Yeah, we got a call from one of the helicopter training officers out at Whiting Field yesterday and he spotted a kayak with our logo on it hidden in a marshy area not far from where Judge Ramsey was shot."

"Really?" Nick's ears perked up. "I assume you retrieved it."

"Yes, sir, and the reason I'm telling you is that two empty 12 gauge shotgun shells were under the seat."

"Still got 'em?"

"In one of them zippered plastic bags. We were careful not to touch 'em. Hasn't rained in a while so might be a print or two left on the shells."

"Never know. We'll check them out. I'll drop by today. Good to hear you got your kayak back, Alex."

Alex gave a disgruntled snort. "Knew we would after I filled out all that dang insurance paperwork. Oh, well, I'll just rip it up now. See you, later."

* * *

Maureen poured hot water from the boiling kettle on the stove into a galvanized tub that sat on the porch. She sprinkled laundry soap on the steaming surface and dumped her soiled clothes into the makeshift washer. It was either clean her laundry in the bay or do it the old-fashioned way.

Otis offered to construct a clothes line. He nailed a spike into an oak tree, walked close to twenty feet to another oak, and repeated the process. Next, he picked up a coil of nylon rope, tied one end to a spike, and strung the rest between the two trees.

"Gotcha someplace to hang your things, Miz Maureen. Just like my mama used to do."

"Thank you. I'm beginning to appreciate how spoiled women are today. Can't imagine doing this a couple times a week for five or six kids."

"You know you don't have to work like this. I can get my cousin Tyrone to drive you into town so's you can use one of them laundry mats."

Maureen shook her head. "Can't take a chance of being recognized."

Otis took back his offer. "Guess I never thought of that. No sense invitin' trouble." A shadow crossed his face. "Got my own with this here ankle bracelet. Reminds me every day."

Maureen scrubbed two socks together and glanced at her friend.

"You won't be wearing it long. Not with Nick on your side. He's doing everything he can to clear your name."

A smile brightened Otis's face. "We's both lucky to have him, Miz Maureen. I don't believe I've ever had a friend like him."

"That makes two of us," replied the red-haired woman with soap suds spattered all the way up to her elbows.

After rinsing her laundry, Maureen carried the clothes to the makeshift line and began to hang them in the sunshine. An uneasy feeling stirred in the bottom of her stomach. Although no one but Otis was at the fish camp, she felt another's presence. She looked around and the crackling of pine needles on the floor of the woods caused her heart to beat faster. Despite the mounting morning temperatures, a chill shook her body.

Is someone watching me? she wondered. Once again, she looked with intent into the maze of ferns, grasses, undergrowth and towering pine and oak trees. *There—behind that thick vegetation. Was that a flash of white? Was it an illusion? The reflection of the sun's rays off a silver saw palmetto? Maybe it's a white-tailed deer scurrying on its way.* Maureen dreaded her next thought. *Or was it a human?*

She wasted no time in finishing her chore and ran back to the house. Once inside, she made a decision. Her eyes fell on the shotgun leaning against the wall in the kitchen behind the door. *Maybe it's time Otis and I did some target shooting. A little practice wouldn't be a bad idea.*

* * *

Owen sat in his pickup on the side of the road and took a drag off his marijuana joint, inhaled, and let the drug linger in his body a few seconds before exhaling. He still had a hard time believing what he saw in his binoculars.

Man, how did Otis get hooked up with the likes of that shapely, good looking broad with flaming red hair? And a white woman! This don't make no sense. Him not outta prison one month. I gotta keep an eye on that brother of mine. Owen chortled. *Might be time to get friendly again. Yes siree, I'll be makin' me a visit.*

Owen looked at his gold-rimmed watch and put the key in the ignition. Sam should be back from lunch by now. Time for a little chat.

* * *

Samuel closed his cell phone and let out a sigh of relief. His ears still rang from the angry outburst he tolerated from Rod. *So Maureen disappeared. Big deal. It's not like she's the only woman on earth. There's plenty to go around as far as I can tell. I've got enough on my plate to worry about without shouldering his personal problems.*

The turn of the doorknob to his office caught Sam's attention and as the door opened a crack, he heard his secretary protest.

"I'm sorry, sir, you don't have an appointment. You can't simply walk in. Mr. Wilson is a busy man."

Sam recognized Owen's voice and walked to the door.

"I'm sorry," the distraught woman looked at her boss with pleading eyes. "But he insists on seeing you." She cast a scornful glance in Owen's direction.

'It's all right. I'll see him." Sam put her concerns at rest, motioned for the man to follow him and closed the door before anyone heard the exchange and called security.

"I told you never to come here," he glared at Owen. "That was part of our agreement."

Owen reached for a leather-covered chair, sat down, spread his legs out before him and wiggled around until he found a comfortable position.

"You and me got business," he declared.

Sam's eyebrows knit together. "What business? You got your money."

"Future business. I'm not getting any younger and its time I started plannin' my retirement."

A ridiculing laugh erupted from inside of Sam. "Retirement? You're joking. When does a drug dealer retire? The only thing that's going to retire you is a bullet."

Owen sat up in the chair and jerked his baseball cap from one side to the other.

"I got me a plan, Mr. State Attorney and you're part of it. I bin doin' your dirty work for years—you and that Yankee friend of yours.

"And you've been well paid for it, too."

"Not complaining."

Sam did not like the direction this conversation was going. He removed his suit jacket and looked at Owen with suspicion. Tension mounted and his fingers twitched. *What does he want?*

Owen came straight to the point. "I know you want to take Judge Ramsey's place, don't ya?"

"I've applied for the position. The committee interviews me in a couple of days. What's that got to do with you?"

A sneer snaked onto Owen's ebony face. "Eighteen years ago there was a certain young assistant State Attorney who didn't do his job. Remember him?"

Owen saw the perspiration form on Sam's brow. "I'm bettin' that committee might like to hear the truth."

Sam reached for his water bottle and took a swig. "And how's that going to happen?"

Owen settled back into the chair and crossed his arms and legs.

"It like this. My cousin Tyrone, he a church man. My family all good Pentecostals."

"What happened to you?"

Irritated, Owen pounded his fist on the arm of the chair. "You gonna keep interruptin' or hear me out? 'Cause I ain't leavin' til you do."

Sam motioned with his hand to continue.

"Like I say, Tyrone never tell a lie. Never do nothin' his mama told him not to do. He came to me the other night—Wednesday after the evening church meetin' and he tells me the Lord bin speakin' to him 'bout me."

Sam started to laugh. "Man, you've been smoking pot this morning, haven't you? I can't wait to hear what the Lord had to say about you."

This time Owen ignored the mockery.

"Tyrone says He told him that I'm to go to Otis and confess that I done him wrong or I'll spend eternity in hell."

Another chuckle came from Sam. "He nailed you on that one! You know where confessing is going to land you, don't you?"

Owen pointed his finger at Sam. "It's you outta be worried. If I talk , there go your chance at the judge's bench and you'll never practice law in Florida again."

The mocking expression on Sam's face turned to anger. "How much? It's blackmail isn't it?"

"Five thousand a month. I can live pretty good on five G's."

"Not from me you won't. The sweat now dripped from Sam's brow and he pulled a white handkerchief from his pants pocket and swiped it across his face.

"Your choice. You got everything to lose—I got nothin'. So what if I get twenty years in prison? The state takes care of me. Pretty good retirement, huh?"

The pink glow around Sam's collar worked its way up his neck to his temples. "Get out of my office you piece of scum."

As Owen started to rise from the chair, he informed Sam, "I've been down to the fish camp to check things out. Watched from the woods. Otis workin' hard to clean the place up. Even got him a woman. A white gal with shiny red hair. Good lookin'. I'm thinkin' hard on this forgiveness thing Tyrone talkin' 'bout. Be in touch, Sam. You know how to find me."

Sam watched as this man with arrogance written all over his face tipped his hat at Mrs. Reynolds and in true southern fashion said, "It's been a pleasure, ma'am."

As the door of his office closed, Sam picked up his cell phone and hit speed dial. At the sound of hello, he uttered three words, "I found Maureen."

Chapter Twenty-Seven

Pools of sparkling sunshine reflected off the waves of tumbling water on Blackwater Bay. *Great day for fishing, Dad*, muttered Nick to himself as he drove up to the marina. *Wish you were here, I'd be tempted to take a day off work and spend it with you like we used to do. But…that's not going to happen, so I'll trek on. Got a lot on my plate with the pressure of the Ramsey case, Maureen in hiding, and our old friend Otis Washington under house arrest. I need one of those 'ah-ha' moments to get a good lead. Hasn't happened yet. Got to regroup and see if I'm missing anything. Maybe these shotgun shells will be the breakthrough we're looking for.*

Alex saw Nick get out of his car and head down the ramp to the docking area.

"Hey, Lieutenant, over here. I want to show you the kayak. We put it aside so no one could rent it until you gave it a goin' over."

"Thanks, I appreciate that. Never know when the smallest piece of evidence can become a big deal. Is it that two-man lime one under the deck?"

"Yep. That's it. Go ahead and check it out while I service this customer."

Nick made his way over to the kayak and took out his tape measure. Four feet from the front seat to the back seat—enough room to hide a shotgun without hindering the ability to paddle. *And what is that sticking to the underside of the back seat? Looks like a piece of paper.* Nick bent down and examined it further. *A Walmart receipt.* Always prepared to take secure evidence, Nick reached into his jacket pocket and extracted a Zip-lock baggie that held a pair of tweezers. He opened the bag, took them out to pick up the paper, and deposited the receipt back in the bag. Through the plastic he saw that someone paid cash for a box of shells.

Nick's adrenaline began to pump. *What's the date?* His eyes scanned the print—March 10/2013. The day Judge Ramsey was shot. *Finally*, he gushed, *some hard evidence.*

By now, Alex was by his side with another baggie containing the two 12 gauge shotgun shells.

"All yours, Lieutenant," he said, handing them over to Nick. "Hope they haven't been contaminated. Maybe your guys can get a clean print. By the way, when the kayak came up missing, we tried to contact the dude who rented it, but he used a bogus name and number."

"Figures," said Nick as he took the shells and stuck them in his side pocket. "Thanks for your cooperation. You can put the kayak back on the rental rack. Nick looked around and continued, "I like the looks of your operation here. Might be persuaded to take up the sport myself one of these days."

"Be happy to oblige, Lieutenant. See you later."

* * *

Nick wasted no time in getting the shells to the lab. The gal who took them gave him a teasing smile.

"I know, Lieutenant, you don't have to tell me—top priority, right?"

"You got it, sweetie. Am I that transparent?"

"After working ten years at this lab, I see who understands the old cliché, the squeaky wheel gets the grease. Will four o'clock be soon enough?"

"I'll be here. Thanks, Lori. How many IOU's does that make?"

"Too many, but who's counting?" She laughed. "Get out of here. I've got work to do."

On his walk back to his office, Nick looked through the glass-paneled door with the words "Sergeant Connor Andrews" written on it and noticed his partner sitting at his computer. Connor's brows knit together in a frown as he gazed at the screen. Anxious to tell him that there may be a small break in the case, Nick rattled the doorknob and walked in.

"Hey, you look serious this morning. What's on your mind?"

"The Ramsey case. Thought I'd make a spread sheet and gather the data we have. Sometimes it helps to see the facts before me. Here," Connor pulled up another chair alongside his and motioned for Nick to take a seat, "read it yourself and see if I've missed anything."

Nick orally read the bullet points:

A. Judge Henry Ramsey— sentencing judge eighteen years ago in the Otis Washington case.
B. Judge Ramsey shot with a 12 gauge shotgun March 10, 2013 two days after Washington's release on a party barge on Blackwater Bay.
C. Otis Washington's prints taken off the barge railing.
D. Tracy Sloan convinced she targeted the wrong man in carjacking.

E. Defense attorney for Washington, Robert Swift, Samuel Wilson and Judge Ramsey meet. State Attorney upset and storms out of meeting.
F. Samuel Wilson encouraged Judge Ramsey to invest in Worldwide Investments, but returns were not favorable and Ramsey sends a letter asking for an investigation by the SEC.
G. Worldwide Investments may be a Ponzi scheme.

Nick reached over the keyboard, and as he started to type, he announced, “As of this morning we can add another bullet to your list.”

Connor, surprised, asked, “Something come up I’m not aware of, boss?”

Nick gave his partner a teasing jab in the ribs. “Gotta get up early to catch the worm. Soon as I came in, Alex from the marina called to tell us that missing rented kayak was found near the crime scene and two spent 12 gauge shotgun shells lay on the bottom of the kayak.”

“Well, now we’re getting somewhere.” Connor straightened his shoulders and his body language begged for more.

“I’ve already retrieved them and the lab is checking for prints. While I was giving the kayak a going over, a small piece of paper caught my eye. It apparently had gotten wet and stuck to the underside of the back seat.”

“So what is it?”

“A receipt from Walmart.”

“So…what’s the relevance? Big deal.”

Nick took on that bulldog face Connor recognized when his partner felt he was on to something.

“Listen, the boys at the marina run an impeccable operation. Those kayaks are sprayed and cleaned from one end to the other and they would never rent one with a speck of trash in it. The receipt must have slipped out of the renter's pocket when he reached for the ammunition. The store will have their copy, so they'll match. The date on this one is March 10,2013."

Connor gave a gasp. "The day Judge Ramsey was murdered."

Nick nodded. "Exactly. Coincidence? Maybe not."

Connor reached for his jacket. "Well, what are we waiting for? The marina kept a contact sheet on each renter. Let's pay the guy a call."

"Alex already tried to contact him when he was late returning the kayak. No such name, number, or address. Dead end."

Connor pounded his fist on the table. "I hate it when a trail starts out hot and turns cold. You got another plan?"

Nick's right hand brazed the side of his shaven cheek and he paused in thought before answering. "I do, but we're going to have to play it cool until the lab can lift a print off the shells. The security tape at Walmart will show everyone who bought ammunition on March 10."

"Man, that's gonna be some lineup. Do you know how many folks are stocking up these days?"

"That's why we need to identify the print. If my hunch is right, I know someone who can recognize the customer we're after."

Chapter Twenty-Eight

Samuel Wilson sat in Rod Santia's cottage staring out the window at the familiar rhythm of the bay. One wave after another glided with ease over another until it reached the sandy shoreline. Seagulls followed the fishing boats, their eyes magnetized to the guts and entrails of the forthcoming feast of various filleted fish.

But Sam's mind was far from the events around him. His lips touched the rim of a crystal wine glass and with one flip of his wrist drained the last drop of Chablis.

As he reached for the bottle to refill his glass, Rod's voice cautioned, "Careful—tomorrow's a big day for you. Can't have the State Attorney show up at the interview hung over expecting to win the vacancy seat on the bench."

Sam's arrogant smile broke the tension. "I'm a shoe-in. My resume' is impeccable—most experienced candidate, five years as an assistant State Attorney, the last six as head State Attorney, highest number of convictions in the last ten years. Besides, I'm a local. Folks trust a local."

Sam ignored the laughing sneer from Rod, who said, "But that's not what's bothering you, is it?"

Despite Rod's warning, Sam poured himself another glass of wine. "You're right."

"He has to go, friend. His time has come and he's no longer an asset. He's turned into a liability. I see it all the time where I come from. People outgrow their usefulness. Owen Washington knows too much. Not only about you but me, too."

Sam agreed. "No doubt about it, but do you know how long I've known him?'

"Doesn't matter. If you start getting sentimental, you'll lose your nerve."

Rod's words appeared to evaporate as Sam continued, "I was fresh out of law school. Nervous, scared to death, and I needed the drugs to keep up my confidence. Somehow I got him acquitted of possession of marijuana and we made a deal. We've been making deals for over twenty years."

Rod's eyes locked into Sam's. "The difference is this will be the last one. The committee meets at five o'clock, remember? He's got you backed in a corner."

Sam was quick to come back. "Don't worry. It's all arranged. Time and place."

"Where?"

"We have a secret meeting place."

"You know I've had experience in this area, so be sure you've covered your bases. Make it a clean shot. Arouse no suspicions. Have an alibi and get out fast. I hear folks shooting all the time around these parts. Must be one of the most populated NRA counties in Florida." Rod snickered at his own comment.

Sam finished his wine, stretched, and started to rise out of the chair, but Rod put out a hand to stop him.

"Before you go, I want to hear what Owen told you about Maureen."

"Owen never mentioned her name. He simply told me his brother has a white woman fitting Maureen's description presumably living at the fish camp. He actually seemed a little jealous."

Rod interjected, "If it's Maureen, that doesn't surprise me. That's all?"

"It makes sense that Melino would hide her there. He's a smart cookie. The place is isolated and run-down, hardly a place to expect to find a lady of her caliber. There's also someone there to keep watch. Let me warn you, you won't get by Otis Washington without a bullet finding you first. This one is more than routine protection for Melino—it's personal.

"That's the part that galls me the most, Sam. I've been to that camp a few times since I've been coming here over the years. I know the inlets to hide in. They'll never suspect I'm on a mission."

Rod gave Sam a manly hug of assurance. "Go home and get some rest. If things go as I plan tomorrow, Maureen and I will be flying out of here in my Cessna before Melino blinks an eye. Keep in touch."

* * *

Half elated but at the same time frustrated, Nick sat on the porch swing at the bay and relayed to Maureen the events of the day.

"But what luck to even get a print off the shells after laying on the bottom of the kayak all this time," encouraged the lady at his side. "The glass is half full, my dear."

Nick squeezed her shoulder and drew her closer. "You're right, Ms. Optimist. I'm just anxious to know if

AIFS has a match in their data base. Thought I'd get results today, but the main computer's shut down."

"Hey, computers get over-stressed, too." Maureen's voice softened. "Be patient."

Nick felt the warmth of her lips press against his. He returned the gesture until a sharp nip on his ankle broke up the embrace. "What the…?"

Instantly, Otis came running around the porch with a dog leash in hand.

"I's sorry, folks, Tyrone's dog had her a litter of seven puppies a couple months ago and he thinks I needs one."

Maureen jumped off the swing and scooped up the bundle of squirming fur. "A Spaniel. Perfect for down here, Otis. They love people and will be happy to live near the water. What's its name?"

"Ain't got no name yet. You name him. He like you, I can tell."

Without hesitation, the word Lucky came out of her mouth. "Because he's lucky to have you as his master, my friend."

"Oh, great," feigned Nick as the puppy spread doggie kisses all over Maureen's face, "now I have competition!"

"No," she protested, "now you've got an extra pair of eyes to watch over me—might keep the bad guy away."

Chapter Twenty-Nine

Connor watched his boss drum the end of his pencil on a blank piece of paper, take a sip of coffee, get up from his chair, and walk around the desk and sit down again.

"Nick," there's nothing you can do to get the results of those prints any faster. I've never seen you so antsy. What's the deal?

"Sorry, pal. I know I'm acting like a kid in school with an attention deficit disorder, but there's something under my skin."

"Wouldn't be a hunch, would it? I believe we've been down this road before." Connor gave Nick one of his knowing smiles.

"Hear me out. If the prints come back with a match to Maureen's old flame, I believe we've got our man. We know Walmart will have their copy of the ammunition receipt I found."

Connor nodded, his interest heightened as Nick continued. "And this is where technology plays its part—security camera."

"You want Maureen to I.D. the guy, right?"

"No." Nick protested. "She may have to, but I don't want her involved at this point. Andy at forensics has seen him twice. I'll have Walmart security run the tape for March 10. Rod Santia will be caught in the act buying the shells."

Connor raised his eyebrows as the whole setup took root. "Okay, the guy had good reason to shoot Ramsey, especially when he found out the SEC has opened an investigation spurred on by the judge. But you know me, Nick, I'm going to shoot holes in your theory so we don't miss anything."

"Take aim, partner."

"The marina boys tell us it was a black man who rented the kayak. The evidence we have came out of that same kayak."

Nick stroked his chin while he pondered Connor's argument. "Santia's style is slick. He lets others do his dirty work so he wouldn't take the chance of being recognized later. Hire a local to rent a two-man kayak—someone who was familiar with the bay and had to know Henry's evening routine with the party barge."

"But then there's a witness to a murder. He'd have to eliminate him, too. According to Otis Washington and forensics, only two shots were fired, and the judge took both of those."

The men sat in silence, each sifting the facts and possible scenarios. After a few minutes, Nick broke the tension. "There could be a third conspirator. I agree, the black guy was probably local. Someone the third party knew because Santia's not familiar with the slime around here."

"And…" Connor's voice grew animated. "He may have been hired to simply transfer the kayak to a particular location and then leave so Santia could finish the job on his own."

Nick's response brought a chuckle from his partner. "Is this scary or what? You're actually starting to think like me."

The ringing phone on the desk cut their levity short. "Melino, here." At once, the strain of the morning changed to one of triumph as Nick listened to Lori read the report generated by the prints. "Yes! Bring me the hardcopy now, please." Nick gave Connor a thumbs up and put the phone back in its cradle.

"Scored again! You got up on the right side of the bed today, partner."

"Finally, something solid. Get out your notepad, Connor. I've got a list of things that need done and done fast. Recruit a couple other fellows on the team to help."

Connor picked up a pen and poised it to write.

"First, put an APB out on Rodney Santia. Then check registration at all the hotels in Escambia and Santa Rosa Counties. Start at the high end ones. He's not the type to travel cheap."

A questioning look crossed Connor's face. "Maureen doesn't know where to find him?"

"I asked her when I took her to the fish camp and she told me she had no idea. Santia didn't reveal his location and she didn't want to know at the time. He could be with an acquaintance, too."

"Yeah, there's no telling at this point, but we'll rat him out into the open. What direction are you going in now?"

Nick picked up the phone and started to dial. "I need Andy to come to Walmart and look at that security tape. Hope he's not in the middle of an autopsy. Without Maureen there these days, I know forensics is short-handed. We need a positive ID today."

Connor threw his coffee cup in the trash, closed his notepad, and started out the door. "I'm pumped. Ready to close in on this guy."

Nick cut him off before he finished. "Call me with even the smallest lead. We can't blow this one!"

* * *

"There." Andy pointed to a tall man handing over cash to the cashier. "The one wearing one of those vests with pockets all over the front. He's the man who spoke to Maureen ."

Nick face was solemn. "You're absolutely sure, Andy? Not a doubt in your mind? Take a closer look."

Andy moved up to the screen "Freeze the tape." His eyes bore into each face, but they came back to the man with camouflage splattered all over the vest. "I'm willing to testify it's the same man, Nick."

"That's a big piece of this puzzle. But let's roll the tape some more. I want to see where he puts the receipt." In seconds, the answer revealed what Nick suspected. "In the largest left front pocket. From what I see, a fella could stash a handful of shells there, too."

"Sure," Andy replied. "I've done it myself out duck hunting. Quicker than fumbling through a box or sack."

Nick turned to the store manager. "I'm going to need this tape for evidence. Go ahead and make a copy for your records, then please call me and I'll come by and get it. Any problem with that?"

"Not that I can see. We'll do anything to help the investigation."

After shaking hands with the manager, Nick and Andy maneuvered their way around several shoppers blocking the aisles.

"Must be a big sale somewhere in this store," remarked Andy. "Looks as though it's going to be a money-making day. That Sam Walton knew what he was doing. Too bad he isn't around today. We could use his brains in Washington."

Nick agreed as he side stepped a runaway toddler. "Don't get me started on politics—we'll never solve this case."

Chapter Thirty

"Lawdy, lawdy," sighed Otis as he watched his new canine companion run helter-skelter among the grasses and bulrushes chasing leaping frogs. "My work's cut out for me. That dog got a mind of his own."

Maureen stopped peeling the potatoes she intended to boil for the potato salad.

"Just like a 'young un'," she replied in her best imitation southern slang. "Gotta get 'em young and train 'em up like the Good Book says so they won't depart from it when they've grown."

Otis looked at her with sad, weary eyes. "Don't always work that way, Miz Maureen." He raised his head toward the sky. "Mama, God rest her soul, died broken-hearted over my brother Owen. You'd think if one twin listen to his mama, the other do the same. Not him. He stubborn—always in trouble. Most of it Mama never even knew about."

"Where is he now?" The last potato plopped into the waiting pot. Little drops of water clung to the metal edge.

"Around and about, I hear. Tyrone run into him in town every so often. He's tryin' to get Owen back in church like in the ole days. Thinks it might turn him around. Otis shook his head. "Ain't gonna happen. Ifin' it did, it'd be a miracle."

"Has he been to see you?"

"Nope. He ashamed. Not once did he come to the prison in all them years to see his brother."

"Why did he stay away?"

"Guilt. 'Cause he know he's the one should have been behind bars. I never hijacked no car. Mr. Nick believes me."

"Can you prove your brother's guilty?"

"Nope. What's done is done. I got a few more good years ahead and I'm movin' on. Some folks never satisfied with what they got—always wantin' more. Not me. I'm happy livin' on the banks of this bay. The Lawd provide everything I need right here. Including the mullet I caught this morning to eat with that tater salad you fixin."

Maureen looked at Otis and surprised him with a secret. "I think you and I have some things in common, my friend. I'm an identical twin, too. My sister Shannon and I have completely different personalities, though. We haven't seen each other in years and there's been no contact."

Otis reached out and patted Maureen's hand. "I knows how that hurt. Was she wild like Owen? Shamed to let the family know where she was and who she with?"

"I know she ran with a wild crowd in high school Left home shortly after graduation. I tried to find her but always came up with a dead end. Heaven only knows where she is now. I haven't mentioned her to Nick. My own story is bad enough."

Otis stood, removed his straw hat and gave his forehead a swipe with his handkerchief. "He won't hear it from me, so don't worry your pretty head about that. I'll be over at the fish-cleaning table if you need me."

Maureen stood up and shielded the sun from her eyes as she looked across the bay.

"Fish must be biting over yonder, Otis. Some guy's been trolling along the inlet all morning."

"I noticed him, too. Hasn't moved much in the last hour. Maybe he'll run out of bait and come buy some from us."

Maureen spent the next hour preparing the potato salad for their evening meal. She enjoyed reviving her cooking skills that she'd abandoned since her days as a wife and mother. The death of her husband and daughter as well as working long hours did little to encourage proper meal preparation. It felt good to feel needed again. She knew both Otis and Nick appreciated her efforts to feed them.

Every now and then Lucky scrambled off the porch in pursuit of a squirrel. It amused Maureen that he never succeeded in capturing one before it dashed up a tree and sat on a branch scolding the pursuer beneath. This time, it was a rabbit that caught Lucky's attention. Bounding from one spot to another in zigzag fashion, the rabbit determined to take the dog on a merry chase—right through a hole in the fence!

"Lucky, come back!" yelled Maureen as the screen door slammed behind her. "Lucky, stop!"

But the dog was intent on catching the teaser in front of him and paid no heed to Maureen's commands. They ran up the sandy side road toward the county asphalt two-lane highway. Clearly in the lead, the rabbit took off into the thick of the woods. Suddenly two shots echoed through the air and Lucky, stunned by the noise, halted at the side of the road.

Maureen, panting to catch a breath, feared for Lucky's safety and grabbed his collar. At the same time, she saw the rear of a white Corvette spin in the sand and take off. Still on the scent of the rabbit, Lucky wiggled and squirmed until he freed himself from Maureen's grasp and headed straight into the woods.

Something's not right, thought Maureen. *Those shots were too close for comfort. Besides, why would a hunter shoot then take off so quickly?*

The intensity of Lucky's barking grew louder and soon it was a continuous howl. Maureen called for him to come to her, but to no avail. Just as she stepped off the road to cross the ditch alongside the woods, Otis appeared a short distance behind carrying his shotgun.

"There you are." Relief washed over his face. "I done almost had a heart attack, Miz Maureen, when I seen you gone. What brings you here?"

"Lucky chased a rabbit from the camp all the way down the road and now he's in there." She pointed to a spot several yards beyond them. And he won't stop whining and barking."

"Did you hear the shots?" asked Otis. "It ain't huntin' season."

"I heard two gunshots over there but no sign of a hunter. Lucky's found something and I'm not feeling good about it."

Before Maureen could stop Otis, he jumped the ditch and barreled through the bushes. She followed behind until Lucky ran up to them, whimpered, and then trotted forward several hundred feet. Lying on his side beneath a pine tree on a bed of long leaf needles was a man clutching his stomach. A wide-brimmed hat hid his face and blood covered his jeans and black hands.

Maureen raced ahead of Otis and knelt down to examine the wound. As she did so, the man's hat fell off and Otis let out a scream. "Owen! My brother. Owen!"

The shock on Otis's face sent fear through Maureen. *How would he react? Less than two hours ago, he admitted there was no love lost between him and his twin.* She looked into his agonized, tear-filled, eyes and spoke softly, "I'm calling Nick. An ambulance will be here, soon."

As she pressed speed dial on her smart phone, Maureen reached for Owen's wrist and felt for a pulse. The internal beat weakened with each breath he took. As she cradled his arm, he opened his eyes and they fell upon Otis who broke down and sobbed against his brother's chest. "Don't die, brother. Don't die. Who done this?"

His voice but a whisper, Owen panted, "Sam…State Attorney." Perspiration dripped off his forehead and he struggled with each syllable. "For…give me, Otis. I…done you…wrong."

* * *

"No Rodney Santia registered at any of the hotels we checked," reported Connor. "So I pulled up the Santa Rosa County Property site."

"Hey, good idea. Any luck?" asked Nick.

Connor handed a hardcopy list of property owners over to his boss. "Look at the highlighted one."

The name and address popped out at once. "So he owns a cabin on the bay." Nick's eyes darted back and forth across the information.

"Notice the location." Connor waited for Nick's response.

"Four lots down from the Ramsey residence. Yes! How convenient. Easy to watch Henry's evening routine. We've got enough to bring him in on suspicion of murder. His place shouldn't be hard to find, but let me grab my county map. Some of these private side roads aren't always well maintained."

The ringing of Nick's cell phone interrupted his search for the map. One glance at the caller's name and number sent a tingle through Nick. "Morning, sweet girl. What's up?"

Maureen's voice bordered on panic. "Nick come quickly. Owen Washington's been shot in the stomach out in the woods. He's dying. Call an ambulance. Otis is a mess."

Connor saw the muscles in his partner's face tighten and heard anxiety in his voice. "Where are you? At the camp? Give me a location."

"In the woods alongside the sandy road that connects to the paved county one. Probably less than a quarter mile from the camp. He's losing blood like crazy. At this rate, he won't last long."

"I'm on my way. Hang in there, baby."

With no time to lose, Nick called 911 and set the wheels of help in motion. Connor picked up the gist of Maureen's call from the bits and pieces he heard coming from Nick to the 911 dispatcher.

"Okay, fill in the blanks for me," he requested. "Something's gone down out at the camp, but who's the victim? Otis?"

"Owen, his twin brother. I'm not surprised. He's been off and on the law's radar for years. Always managed to slip through the hoops."

Nick checked his jacket pocket for his notepad and pen. I'm out of here, but I want you to call forensics, give them the directions, and get a couple of patrol cars out there as well. See you. We'll have to deal with Santia later."

Nick's Camaro wasn't too far behind the ambulance. He came to a sudden stop on the shoulder of the road when he saw the flashing lights and a redheaded woman flailing her arms in the air as she motioned for the EMT's to follow her into the woods.

Nick took up a position in the rear, his eyes darting all around him to take in the surrounding crime scene. Outdoor crime environments presented their own set of problems with weather, terrain, and both animal and human intruders. His team needed to work fast to search for any clues.

By now, Lucky had calmed down and sat beside his master who clung to his brother's hand. As if in a trance, Otis repeated his mantra, "Lawd, please have mercy. Let him live. Let him live. I know he done wrong. Please forgive him."

Nick walked over and put his arm around his friend's shoulder. The resemblance between the twins caught Nick's attention. Their broad nose and chiseled, high cheek bones matched perfectly. He saw how easily one could be mistaken for the other. A flash of gold on Owen's wrist caught Nick's eye—a bracelet with a medical alert symbol embedded among the links.

As the EMT's discussed the best way to get the man on the stretcher, Nick pulled out his cell phone and started to take photos of Owen and the surrounding area.

"Can't wait for forensics," he explained to Maureen.

"I took a few myself with mine while we waited for the ambulance," she returned. "Never hurts to have extra."

Owen's body jerked and he cried out in pain as the two men from the ambulance lifted him onto the stretcher. Otis refused to leave his brother's side and when the ambulance doors opened, he pleaded with Nick to let him go to the hospital, too.

"I can't let you go by yourself. You know you're under house arrest."

"Please, Nick, I can't let him die alone. Mama never forgive me. She always tell me, "You came first. You take care of your brother.'"

Nick pursed his lips and his brows knit together. He looked at Maureen and saw not only a face full of empathy, but a tear trickle down her cheek. Without saying a word, she convinced Nick to compromise. He turned to Otis and said, "I'll go with you. Get in my car."

Maureen walked over and squeezed Nick's arm. "Thank you," she whispered.

"I don't like leaving you alone, but it's not a good idea to be seen in town either."

"Stop worrying. I want to be here when forensics start their work. I know they need help." Suddenly words rushed from Maureen's lips. "In all this excitement I almost forgot something important. Write this down Nick."

Without hesitating he complied. "Okay, what is it?"

"I saw the rear of a white Corvette take off just as I caught up to Lucky. Couldn't make out the driver."

"Connor and a couple deputies should arrive any minute. Tell him to be sure and get a cast made of the tire tracks. I'll call when we know more about Owen's condition." Nick turned his head toward the ambulance then put a kiss on Maureen's cheek. "Be careful."

* * *

The screaming ambulance siren cleared the highway of obstructing traffic and the vehicle stopped in front of the Santa Rosa Medical Center emergency entrance. The EMT's sprang into action and before Nick and Otis had time to park and exit the car, Owen disappeared behind closed doors. Scattered around the waiting room sitting on uncomfortable plastic chairs were worried parents holding crying babies, pale-faced unruly toddlers, and a couple of teenagers texting on smart phones.

The initial smell of dried blood, antiseptics, ammonia, and human perspiration combined to assault one's nostrils. Otis, unfamiliar with the scent, felt his stomach lurch. His eyes searched the room for his brother and he asked, "Where's he at, Nick?"

"Behind those swinging doors with a triage team. They'll look at him first to determine his injuries. With the wounds Owen has, he'll get immediate attention. I need to talk to the E.R. doctor and give him what information we have. You take a seat here in the waiting room and don't move."

"But Nick, I…"

The look on Nick's face sent a message that read, "Back off. No room for argument."

After a short consultation with the doctor, Nick sat beside his despondent friend and said, "I'm curious about something, Otis."

"What that?"

"For eighteen years you carried a grudge when it came to your brother. You swore up and down he did you wrong. Now I see a complete change of heart. I'm confused."

Otis sat with his head bent low. Unbridled tears flowed from his eyes, down his cheek bones, and spattered on the tile floor. His shoulders trembled and he stumbled over his words. "I…I can't rightly explain it. Soon's I saw Owen in terrible pain laid out on the ground grabbin' his stomach…blood runnin'everywhere…all the hate left me. Like da Lawd filled me with forgiveness."

Nick pulled a white handkerchief from his breast jacket pocket and handed it to the weeping man who used it to wipe his face before he continued.

"I believes now that's what Mama want me to do. Bin fightin' it for a long time, but I guess this what it took for me to let it go. Hard lesson to learn for two brothers."

Nick gave his affirmation in the form of a shoulder hug and they sat in silence for the next twenty minutes, each absorbed in their own thoughts until the doctor approached them.

"Gentlemen, Mr. Washington is being prepped for surgery. He's conscious at the moment and insists on talking to his brother." Dr.Porter looked at Otis. "Says you have to hear him out."

Nick nudged Otis's arm. "This may be a confession that clears your name. It's important that there be witnesses. Dr.Porter and I need to be with you. Do you have any objections?"

Otis squared his shoulders. "Lead the way, doctor."

Behind a curtained off portion of the emergeny room, a nurse stood beside the bed and kept a watchful eye on the monitors. At the sound of shuffling feet, Owen opened his eyes. A weakened hand reached out for his brother. Otis took it and held it to his chest. As Nick flipped his notepad open and prepared to write, the nurse left and in a strained whisper, Owen made his confession.

"I let you take blame for the car jackin' Otis. The police mistake you for me. After the crash, I ran and hitched a ride to Mobile. For years I bin Sam Wilson's drug supplier. That's why he quick to put you away." Again Otis let the tears flow without any attempt to wipe them off his moistened face.

Owen's energy wavered, but after a pause and a deep breath, he indicated he wasn't finished. "I knows a lot about the State Attorney—bad things he don't want no one to find out. He shot me. I shoulda knowed he would."

Nick leaned closer, repulsed by the words crossing a dying man's lips.

"He in tight with the man from up north. They hire me to rent a kayak and leave it hidden in the bushes, but it weren't me who kill the judge. One of them did."

By now, Owen struggled to take a breath. Dr. Porter glanced at the monitor and a frown wrinkled his brow. He looked at Nick and said, "We need to get him into surgery. Now."

As Nick closed his notepad and put it back into his jacket pocket, he looked at Otis and saw the man cling to his brother's hand. He refused to let go. As hard as it was emotionally for him, Nick reached over and pried black fingers from black fingers.

"I loves you, Owen. Just like Mama always told me—you's my brother." The tremor in Otis's voice elicited a wave of sympathy and a tear clouded Nick's vision.

Without further conversation, the medical team whisked Owen into an elevator up to a waiting surgical theater. Forty-five minutes later, a grim faced doctor took Otis's hand and gave him the news.

"The bullet shattered his liver and he bled to death."

Chapter Thirty-One

No sooner had Nick, Otis, and the ambulance left for the hospital when two patrol cars and the forensic van pulled off the road and parked on the shoulder. Once more, Maureen led the way into the crime scene.

"Hey, great to see you," said Andy giving his fellow worker a big hug. "Thought you'd want in on the action so I threw in a coverall for you, too."

"Wouldn't miss it. My skills will need honing if I don't get back to work soon. I have to admit, though, the rest has been great."

"You let Nick decide when it's best for you to come out of hiding, Maureen," offered Connor. He seems to have a sixth sense about these things."

Maureen laughed. "Oh, I agree he's one of a kind." Her voice grew tender and a pink blush colored her cheeks. "But one of the best kind."

Connor and the deputies combed the woods for anything the killer may have left behind. They also took photos of the oversized tire prints and used plaster of Paris to copy the imprints left in the sandy road. Maureen and her team took their own photos and collected blood samples that pooled in the pine straw. One of the deputies found an empty bullet casing that looked like it came from a .38 caliber pistol.

After an hour, they all decided their work was complete and packed up to leave.

"Sure you don't want me to drive you down to the camp, Maureen?" asked Connor. "You must be tired after all this excitement."

"Nah, I'm fine. Besides, I've got Lucky to handle. He's a live wire and needs to run off some of that energy. Thanks, anyway. Take care guys."

Once on their way, Lucky took off down the road eager to get back to the bay. Every now and then he'd run back to Maureen, bark as if coaxing her to go faster, then head for the water. As the pier came into view, Maureen saw Lucky sniffing and checking out a man sitting on the bow of his boat. He wore a large-brimmed straw hat and his face was shaded.

Hmm, thought Maureen, *I wonder if that's the man who fished all morning across from the camp. Maybe he does need to buy some bait.*

Without giving it a second thought, she walked up to him and asked, "May I help you?"

Slowly, a hand pushed back the hat's brim and revealed a face Maureen hoped she'd never see again. For an instant her body froze and she couldn't speak.

"Time you got back. I've spent the whole day waiting for this opportunity. One hand pulled a .380 hand gun from a pocket in his cargo shorts. We're going for a ride. Get in the boat."

Maureen's tongue felt as though it were glued to the roof of her mouth. Finally she managed to sputter, "How did you find me?"

"Come now, Maureen, you know me better than that. I always get what I want—or did you forget? I'm not leaving without you, so get in the boat."

Maureen took small steps forward. There was no escape, especially with water on all three sides of them. She stepped into the bass boat and sat down on the seat."

Before Rod pushed the boat away from the pier, he demanded, "Let me have your phone."

Maureen hesitated. *It's my lifeline*, she wanted to scream. *You can't have my only connection to Nick*. But she knew better than to taunt this man. With trembling hands, she took the phone off the lanyard that hung around her neck and unobtrusively let her thumb press the redial button on its face before handing it to Rod. With one swift throw, he threw it in the bay. Maureen watched as it left a small ripple in the water.

I hate you, the words in her mind translated to a look of pure distain on her frightened face.

"Cheer up, my dear. You used to enjoy flying with me. By tonight you'll be back in Boston."

With a touch of the motor's ignition button, the boat lurched forward. Maureen watched the fish camp grow smaller and smaller until it was no more than a spot in the distance.

Chapter Thirty-Two

The clock on Nick's Camaro read 2:30 p.m., but to Nick this day felt as though it would never end. Santia was still at large, Owen Washington was dead, and a crooked State Attorney allegedly killed him.

But didn't I see Samuel Wilson's picture in the paper this morning? He's a contender in the process to appoint a new judge to fill Ramsey's seat on the bench. Interviews are scheduled to start today at five this afternoon at the courthouse. Well, this is one candidate who will be out of the running.

The Gator jingle on Nick's smart phone rang as he produced it from his jacket pocket. A quick glance at the face told him it was Connor. It also showed he'd missed a call from Maureen. *Why didn't I hear that?*

"Connor, I'm glad you called. Owen didn't make it and I'm driving Otis home. We got a deathbed confession that Samuel Wilson killed him. All these years sucking up the public's trust and then having the gall to think he could take Ramsey's place. Nothing but a piece of slime. I can't wait to put the cuffs on him! Say, somehow I missed a call from Maureen. Everything okay at the camp?"

"Far as I know. We finished up at the crime scene and I offered to drive her back, but she insisted she had the dog and wanted to walk. She's probably anxious to know about Owen."

"Yeah, we were busy at the hospital and I guess I didn't hear it. I'll give her a call now. Maureen told me at the scene she saw a white Vette high tail it out on the sandy road shortly after she heard the shots fired."

Connor jumped into the conversation. "Everyone around town's seen Wilson driving one of those. We took tire prints, so between a witness and the prints it's a no-brainer linking his car to the scene. Guess he wasn't counting on anyone walking along that piece of deserted road mid-morning."

Nick agreed. "Apparently not. He sure picked the wrong woods to pull off a murder. I'm wondering if it wasn't a rush job. Not much planning. Know what I mean?" A detached tone in Nick's voice revealed his true feelings. "Anyway, it's his problem. Ours is to find the evidence we need to arrest him. I'll be back in the office to type up a 'no-knock' search warrant as soon as I get Otis settled down. Call Judge Allen and tell him we're coming in for a warrant."

Nick glanced at Otis, who hadn't said a word since leaving the hospital. His chin touched his chest and his shoulders sagged in defeat. *He's grieving,* thought Nick. *Better to leave him alone.*

Nick's fingers slide over the face of his phone and without hesitation sought Maureen's number. He waited to hear the soft tone of her voice, but instead he heard an automated voice say, "I'm sorry. No one is available to take your call. At the sound of the tone, please record your message."

Hmm, must have dialed wrong. This time, he made sure each number he pressed was correct. Again the automated voice repeated the same message. *Strange, she never mentioned having phone problems. Oh, well, we're almost at the camp.*

Lucky met the car with his usual nonstop barking. At the sight of Otis, he ran circles around him and begged to be petted. Nick ignored the dog and looked around for Maureen. She was nowhere in sight. Normally, she'd be out to the car by now. An uncomfortable feeling sent Nick running into the cabin as he called her name. No answer. Panic drove him to the water. *Could she have fallen into the bay and drowned?* He scanned every inch of shoreline and saw nothing unusual.

"Maureen's not here, Otis! There's something wrong. She'd never leave without telling me."

"Oh, no! Nick, it's my fault. Never should have left the camp, but my brother he need me…"

"Look, we're not going to point fingers at anyone. There has to be a reasonable explanation. Listen, I want Tyrone to stay with you tonight. Your family has to plan a funeral for Owen. The hospital needs to know when to release the body to a funeral home. You got a number for Tyrone?"

"It written down in the kitchen. Don't know why 'cause I never did have a phone. Otis came back with a paper in hand. "You gotta dial him for me, Nick. I don't know nothin' 'bout these things. And my eyes done cried too much to see the numbers."

After a quick conversation with Tyrone's wife, she assured Nick the family would take Otis under their wing. "Least we can do for him," she sighed. "He been through so much."

Nick relayed the message, told Otis his business in town could not wait, and jumped back into the Camaro.

"You gonna look for Miz Maureen?"

"If I have to search every inch of this county. Later, friend."

The engine of his car fired up and Nick shifted into reverse when Otis came running after him flailing his arms.

"Stop. I thought of somethin'. Might be important."

"Tell me, quick."

"This mornin' a man was fishin' across from the camp for quite a while. Every now and then he start the motor and troll along the shore then come back and throw the anchor in."

"What kind of boat and motor?"

Otis answered without a moment's hesitation. "Bass boat. I knows one when I sees one. Had a twenty horsepower Mercury on the back. They has a purr like no other outboard."

"Was the man close enough to get a good look at him?"

Otis shook his head and his initial excitement dissipated. "Too far from the camp to see his face. Besides he was wearing a straw hat with a wide brim. He look tall, though, when he stood to pull the anchor up. Ain't much to go on, huh?"

Nick gave him a smile. "Anything's a start in my job. Now you go in and wait for your kin. Someone will be here shortly."

* * *

The pressure of the present circumstances weighed heavily on Nick. Every minute that passed meant Maureen could be Rod Santia's hostage. *That's the only logical conclusion. Somehow he managed to get to her. But how? He's smart enough to know I'd put an APB out and there's no way he'd get her past Pensacola Airport Security.*

Nick dialed his partner to give him the latest news.

"Maureen's missing and her phone is not accepting calls. I've got a gut feeling she's been kidnapped."

"No way! I'm sorry, partner. I should've insisted she ride with me? I let you down."

"Hey, we don't know what happened and I sure don't want to waste time playing the blame game, so here's what I want you to do. Pick up Evans and go out to Santia's property. You seemed to know how to get there when we discussed picking him up this morning. My guess is that he's gone, but check everything—especially, the boathouse. Get the type of boat and brand of motor. If the motor on his boat is warm, then he hasn't been gone long. Take a photo of any tire tracks in the driveway. They may give a clue as to what he's driving. Connor, be careful—he's dangerous."

"Gotcha. Just got off the phone with Judge Allen. I told him the warrant will specify a weapon and any other incriminating evidence."

"Good. I'll have it ready to be signed in thirty minutes. I don't want Wilson suspicious that we're on his tail, so a search needs to be done before he leaves the courthouse. I'll take a couple deputies with me."

As Nick drove to the edge of town, a small plane buzzed overhead. Something Maureen told him suddenly popped into his mind, *"He even took me flying in his private plane."*

Yes, why not? While we're wasting our time searching everywhere down here, he's off in the clouds heading north. The Milton-T Airport is the closest one to Blackwater Bay. My guess is he has a hangar there. Nick looked at his watch. *No time to drive over there before I get the search warrant.*

Frustrated that everything was happening at once, Nick drew on his experience and focused his whirling thoughts. *Searching Wilson's place comes first. If I'm right about Santia, it will take him eight to nine hours to fly to Boston, so we can buy some time there. Verify with Milton Airport Santia rented hangar space. What type plane? When did he file a flight plan? Contact the FBI and have them stationed not only at Logan International but the smaller airports surrounding the city.* A labored sigh gave away his feelings. *In over twenty-eight years on the force, I can't remember a day as hectic as this.*

Back in his office, Nick made a copy of Owen's confession and signatures of the witnesses. A quick call to the techs confirmed the plaster cast prints turned out well.

"I need to include the tire print photos and the cast ASAP as additional evidence to support the warrant," he explained to the technician.

"Be right over, Lieutenant."

Used to requesting search warrants, Nick listed the specific areas and objects he hoped to find—weapon, clothing, cell phone—anything else that was relevant to the crime.

In less than fifteen minutes, he headed down to the courthouse. The First Baptist church on the corner of Highway 90 rang their bells on the hour. After the third one, Nick jumped out of his car and slammed the door as he looked for a white Corvette in the State Attorney's designated parking space. *Good. He's still here. No time to waste.*

Chapter Thirty-Three

Judge Allen awaited Nick's arrival. Shocked at the request to search the State Attorney's residence and car for a murder weapon, he read the confession and looked at the cast and tire print photos. Without question, the judge signed the warrant, then Nick and his team headed for Samuel Wilson's residence.

One of the deputies jimmied the door open and the search began. They looked in cupboards, drawers, on shelving, in closets, under beds, and even combed the yard for signs of disturbed grass where a .38 could be buried. Nothing produced the evidence they sought. After forty-five minutes, a deputy called out, "Got something, Lieutentant."

Nick rushed into the bedroom hoping to find a revolver, but instead was presented with a Zip-lock bag of marijuana. Disappointed but not discouraged, he asked, "Where'd you find this?"

"Under a loose tile in the shower. Guess Washington wasn't lying about supplying Wilson with drugs."

"You're right. It gives credibility to the confession, so we'll consider it evidence." Nick gave a sigh. "I have a feeling we're wasting our time here looking for the weapon, but there's still a possibility it's in his car."

Nick looked at one of his men and said, "Hanover, get hold of Tom over at his tire shop and tell him this is an emergency. We're trying to beat the clock and we need his expert opinion on a set of tire prints. Meet us behind the courthouse in the parking lot."

"Yes, sir."

Nick turned to the remaining deputy and gave him a sly grin. "You're pretty handy at opening locked doors. How 'bout Corvettes? ZR-1's to be specific."

The deputy chuckled, "It'll be a first but I'm game. Got my Slim Jim in the patrol car. Probably as close as I'll ever get to putting my hands on one of those honeys with my salary."

"Or mine," offered Nick as he pulled his cell phone out of his jacket pocket. "Hey, take one last walk-through while I call my partner. I want him to meet us there."

Connor answered on the first ring. "Santia's gone, Nick. Looks like he left in a hurry, too—a couple of canvas chairs on the deck each still held an empty glass, so we've brought them in for prints. One has a lipstick smudge on the side. Apparently, he entertained a woman recently. There's some fishing gear leaning against the side of the cabin and weeds tangled in the prop of the motor. It's cold so he's been gone awhile."

Nick muttered his frustration under his breath then continued, "I have a feeling he and Maureen are flying his Cessna to Boston. I remembered she told me he owned a plane, but it'll take him a few hours. In the meantime, we have to bring Wilson in. Meet us at the courthouse. No gun found at his home, so it probably is in his car."

"We'll be back in town in twenty minutes." Excitement mounted in Connor's voice. "Can't wait to search that Vette."

Nick laughed, "You may have to take a number and stand in line. The other guys are itching to do the same."

* * *

At 4:15 p.m., Nick's team gathered around Wilson's Corvette. A quick glance at his watch sent his adrenaline racing. He had forty-five minutes to find the evidence he needed to convict Wilson before the Judicial Nominating Committee started the interviews.

As Tom got down on his knees to examine the tires, Nick handed him the photos and the plaster cast. Silence followed as all eyes watched with anticipation. Finally, Tom spoke. "Don't see many of these around—not much call for 'em in this town, but I have a few clients with money to spend. Yep. The tread matches the cast perfectly." A chorus of 'yes' came from the team.

"Look at the width of that tire," commented one of the deputies. "Don't believe I've seen one that wide."

Tom was quick to explain. "This car has 638 Horsepower under the hood. In order to get all that power to the road, they designed a tire with tread that has narrower grooves. See, they're not as deep in order for traction to provide a solid connection to the road. Gives better control." Tom ran his fingers over the surface of the right back tire. "Only problem is they tend to hydroplane in wet weather. Driving this baby takes some skill."

"So we can count on you as an expert witness in court?" inquired Nick.

"You bet, Lieutenant. Always ready to help the law."

"Thanks, Tom. We'll keep in touch. Okay Hanover, see what you can do with that Slim Jim."

The deputy maneuvered the device with skill and soon the sound of a door opening brought a sigh of relief to all involved. Connor wasted no time in delving onto the front seat and scanning the interior. The glove compartment contained nothing but a tire gauge and a registration card. The console held a pair of sunglasses.

"Nothing up front," he called. "Let's lift the seat, guys."

"Pop the trunk, first," Nick instructed as he waited behind the car. With ease his hands lifted the metal and his eyes fell upon a black garbage bag. "We may have something here, fellas." Nick pulled a pair of gloves from his pocket, stretched them over his hands, and gingerly opened the bag. At once, his nostrils twitched and he recognized the smell of blood. His hand reached down into the bag and extracted a white polo shirt with splotches of drying blood across the mid section. Again, Nick felt inside the bag and this time, as he pulled up its contents, a revolver fell out from a rolled up pair of tan pants stained with spots of blood.

"Looks as though we got here before our State Attorney had time to dispose of the evidence. Guess he didn't count on a stomach wound blasting him with the victim's blood. I think I know why, too."

"Fill in the blanks, partner."

"Think of it. He's ready to take aim and suddenly Otis's dog comes barking up the road. He probably meant to shoot Owen in the heart but panics, pulls the trigger, and misses his aim."

Connor shook his head in agreement. "Sounds logical to me. When are we going in to make the arrest?"

Nick looked at his watch. "The committee is convening in five minutes. Connor, take the evidence back to forensics and have them match the blood to Owen's, then get the gun to ballistics."

"A .38 casing was found near the victim, so we've got a match there," offered Connor.

"Evans, come with me. Hanover park the patrol car closer to the back door. We don't need to attract attention in front when we bring Wilson out." Nick looked from one man to the other with praise. "Good work, team. Let's hope the last phase goes as well."

Nick knew he cut it close. He ran up the courthouse steps with Evans close behind, opened the door, and flashed his badge at security. Unsure of where the Judicial Nominating Commission intended to meet, he asked the receptionist at the front desk.

"Second floor in the judge's conference room. But sir, I'm afraid it's a closed meeting."

"Ma'am, this is a police matter. Urgent. Please call the chair person and let me speak to whoever's in charge."

The young woman gave Nick a thorough scrutiny before she dialed the extension.

"Sir, please excuse the interruption, but there's a Lieutenant Melino from the Santa Rosa Sheriff's Office who says he needs to speak to you at once."

"Yes, he does know you are conducting interviews but he's insistent."

A moment of silence passed. "Yes, Mr. Hartle, here he is."

Nick took the receiver and pleaded his case. "Sir, please delay your proceedings until I get up to your room. Believe me, the commission needs to hear what I've got to say." A moment's pause sent the nerves in Nick's fingers to tapping the receptionist's desk. Finally, he received the permission he needed to proceed.

The elevator door opened at the second floor. The men walked down the marble hallway searching for the conference room. Two men dressed in suits sat on either side of a massive oak door flipping through notes as though they were cramming for a final exam. *Good,* thought Nick, *Wilson must be the first candidate on the hot seat.* A smirk creased the edges of his lips. *I've got a few questions to ask him myself, but they aren't the kind he's expecting from the Commission.*

Without being asked, Nick showed his badge to the security guard at the door. "I'm expected." he said.

"Yes, sir. I was told to let you in." He offered to open the door.

All nine members of the Judicial Nominating Commission stopped their informal chatter and looked at Nick with questioning eyes as he approached the chairman. Shock registered on the tenth man's face and he fidgeted from one side of his chair to the other. Like leaking air from a deflated balloon, the color drained from Samuel Wilson's face. He refused to look at Nick.

"Please excuse this interruption, ladies and gentlemen, but I'm here to arrest Samuel Wilson on charges of murdering Owen Washington. The victim died of gunshot wounds at approximately one-fifteen this afternoon."

A unified gasp echoed around the oval table. All eyes turned toward the State Attorney. "What kind of sick joke is this, Melino? I have a solid alibi. Call my hair stylist. At one-twenty she cut my hair."

Nick pulled his notebook from his left jacket pocket and flipped through pages until he found the information he'd written earlier. "I didn't say he was shot at one-fifteen, I said he died at one-fifteen after giving a deathbed confession to Dr. Wayne Porter at the Santa Rosa Medical Center, myself, and Otis Washington, Owen's brother. Both men are willing to sign an affidavit. A couple living in the area heard the shooting, so we have a time frame."

Wilson's eyebrows shot up and his face muscles tensed. Before he had time to retort, Nick read him his Miranda rights and retrieved a pair of hand cuffs secured to his belt.

"Hands behind your back—you know the routine." Nick was none too gentle and the click of the metal locking Wilson's hands together sounded like music to his ears.

A snarl gurgled in the State Attorney's throat and he threatened, "Get ready for a lawsuit, Melino. Once my lawyer gets through with you…"

Again Nick cut him off. "Bring it on because you're also charged as an accomplice to Judge Ramsey's murder."

This time, a mixture of male and female voices erupted throughout the room. Each one horrified at the scene before them.

"What? I can't believe it!" commented one woman. "Get that man out of here," ordered a lawyer. "He's a disgrace to our profession."

At the sound of raised voices, the security guard opened the door and Nick beckoned him to come in.

"I need you to call up a couple of your buddies from downstairs and escort Mr. Wilson to a waiting patrol car. I busted up the chairman's meeting and I owe him a good explanation."

Stymied by the turn of events, Wilson's face, red with rage, turned to Nick and gave him a look that sent chills throughout Melino's body. *Bring it on*, thought Nick. *I can't wait to see you in court.*

Chairman Hartle hurried over to Nick's side. "What's going on, Lieutenant? We need an explanation."

"I understand, sir, but I prefer to talk to you privately."

"Of course." Hartle turned to his peers. "This meeting is adjourned until further notice. Someone please inform the waiting candidates."

Without further adieu, the room emptied and Nick explained everything that transpired since the shooting, including the bloody clothes and weapon found in Wilson's car.

"I'm in total shock!" exclaimed Hartle. "But then one never knows who will fall from grace. A little power can be a dangerous thing. I appreciate your swiftness, Lieutenant. Who knows? We may have voted him onto the bench today."

"Just part of the job, sir, but I need to go. I don't want a crowd to gather downstairs, and he needs to be booked."

While the booking process was in progress, Nick nabbed Connor and drove toward Milton-T Airport. He needed to confirm that Santia rented a hangar and flew off in a plane earlier in the day. Every time he thought of Maureen in the air with Santia, his stomach churned.

"Connor, find me the number of the Boston FBI headquarters on your smart phone. If my hunch is true, I need to have them disperse their agents around the smaller airports in the area ready to meet Santia's plane."

"You don't think he'd fly into Logan International?"

"No. He'd have to file a flight plan. My guess is that he doesn't want a paper trail, but would come in as unobtrusively as possible—fly VFR."

As they drove into the airport parking area, the sound of helicopter blades slicing through the air attracted Connor's attention. "Now that's my idea of fun! Those pilots at Whiting field must have a great time."

"Yeah, until they're sent to combat. Something tells me it's not the same as flying around Santa Rosa County."

"Good point."

The young woman at the office met the detectives at the door with her purse slung over her shoulder.

"Sorry, the office hours are seven a.m. 'til six p.m."

Connor whipped out his badge. "Ma'am, we really need some information. It's very important, and I promise it won't take long."

The curly-headed twenty-something gave a sigh and relented. "Okay, but I've got a date in thirty minutes. Whatcha need?"

Nick took over. "We need to know if a man by the name of Rodney Santia rented a hangar recently."

Curly Head walked to the file cabinet and thumbed through the names. In seconds, she pulled out a folder and opened it. "Yes, sir. He paid in cash for a month's space. Cessna Conquest. Came in today and closed out the account."

"What time?"

"Oh, around noon. I just finished my lunch. Had a pretty red head with him."

Nick was beside himself. "Did he say where they were going?"

"Nah. But wait. Danny, one of our mechanics, is still here working on an engine. He fueled this guy's plane and he might know. Let me get him." She opened a side door and yelled, "Hey, Danny, come here. A couple of detectives want to talk to you."

A tall, thin, young man in grease-covered overalls walked in with a puzzled look on his grimy face.

Nick put him at ease. "No problem, son, just need to know if the man who asked you to fuel his Cessna Conquest this noon told you where he was flying."

"I remember him—one of those pushy type. Told me to hurry and top off the tank. Said he was flying straight through VFR to some place up north close to Boston."

"Will one tank of fuel get him there or will he have to refuel somewhere?" asked Connor.

Danny did some calculations out loud. "A Cessna Conquest holds 370 gallons and flies at 250 knots, so it'll take six to seven hours if the weather's good. Yeah, he can make it, but not much fuel to spare."

Nick thanked Danny for his help and handed his car keys to Connor. "You drive. I need to contact the FBI immediately. Pull up that number on your phone and hand it to me, please. It's an hour later on the east coast so we're working against time."

On the third ring, he got through to the receptionist and asked to speak to an agent on duty.

"Agent Graham. How may I help you?"

"Yes, sir, this is Lieutenant Nick Melino of the Santa Rosa County Sheriff's Office. A man by the name of Rodney Santia allegedly murdered a judge in Milton, Florida, recently and is flying into the Boston area tonight. He has kidnapped a woman and they should land in about two hours. He did not file a flight plan, so I'm sure he plans to land at a smaller airport outside Boston."

"You said Rodney Santia, right?"

"Yes."

"That name is well known in the underground world up here and we've been alerted by the SEC that they want to question him concerning a Ponzi scheme."

"Yes, yes," replied Nick. "He's the one. We can't let him slip through our fingers. I know this is short notice, but everything let loose this morning. He's flying VFR, but he'll have to talk to a tower to get clearance to land. I just don't know what airport he's chosen."

"No problem. We'll notify the surrounding towers to give us that information as soon as he contacts a tower. Our boys will be there to welcome him home."

"Please call my personal cell as soon as you have him in custody. Any hour. I'll be waiting." Nick gave the agent his cell phone number. "The woman's name is Maureen O'Shanesey and she's a medical examiner for the county. I need to talk to her as well. Appreciate your help."

"We're on the same team, Lieutenant. Talk to you later."

Nick looked at Connor with concern and asked, "Did I cover all the bases? This waiting is going to be torture."

Connor reached over and gave his partner a reassuring pat on the arm. "There's nothing more you can do. I know this one is tearing you up personally, but keep the faith, partner. She'll be back here soon. It's been quite a day hasn't it?"

"One for the books. No doubt about that."

Chapter Thirty-Four

Too fatigued to eat, Nick flopped down into his Lay-Z-Boy chair and fell asleep. Every so often he woke with a start and checked his phone to be sure he hadn't missed the FBI's call. He finally turned on the TV and surfed the channels, but nothing caught his interest. All of his thoughts were on the woman he loved. How could this have happened? How did Santia figure out where she was? *Please keep her safe, Lord.* His prayer barely crossed his lips when his cell phone's Gator jingle sent his pulse racing.

"Melino residence."

"Nick this is Tim Graham, FBI."

"Been waiting for your call, Tim. Tell me some good news."

"Two hours ago, we got word that Santia asked for clearance from the tower at Norwood Memorial Airport. We had agents on the ground in anticipation that would be Santia's airport of choice. I have to tell you his welcome home party was not what he expected."

Nick let out an audible sigh of relief before he asked, "And Maureen, is she all right?"

Tim chuckled, "Why don't you ask her yourself. I believe she's anxious to talk to you. I know it's late and we need to get this guy into custody, so I'll talk to you tomorrow. We need more detailed information Later, okay?"

"Thank you, Tim. Excellent work."

A moment of silence passed as Maureen took the phone, then an explosion of words erupted from her sweet mouth. "Nick, I was so scared. He threatened all kinds of things if I didn't cooperate. If you hadn't contacted the FBI, I don't know what would have happened." Nick heard her voice crack with a sob and he pictured the tears running down her cheeks.

His heart warmed at the raw emotion he heard in her voice. "You're safe now, baby. I wish I were there to comfort and put my arms around you, but I promise I'll make it up to you when you get back."

With a stronger voice, Maureen said, "Agent Graham asked me if I'd stay tomorrow and give them a deposition. I've got lots to tell them. I'm staying with his family so I won't be alone.

"Good. I'll arrange for you to pick up a plane ticket at Logan when you're ready for one. I know they're waiting for you so we'll talk tomorrow. Love you, Maureen."

Her response was a soft whisper, but he heard every word. "I love you, too."

Nick sent a short text to both Connor and the Sheriff, then headed for bed. Exhaustion mixed with relief knocked him out cold.

* * *

"Mornin' Lieutenant," greeted Officer Charlie. "Hear you brought in a big fish yesterday."

The color in Nick's neck reddened. "You might say that."

"It's time he was caught. That Wilson is a sly one. Never did trust someone who thinks they're the top dog."

"Maybe a night spent behind bars has changed his attitude. You think?" A smirk creased the corners of Nick's lips.

"Wouldn't want to hold my breath, sir. Oh, I almost forgot. The Sheriff wants you to drop by his office as soon as you can."

"Thanks. I'll get on back there before something else comes along. Have a good one."

The door to Kendall's office was open, so Nick paused then gave a rap on the frame. The Sheriff was focused on his computer screen, but when he heard the noise, he looked up and extended a handshake. He was all smiles. "Your team outdid themselves again, Melino. Two kingpins in one day. Terrific! Wait 'til the governor hears this."

"Getting the bad guys is written in the job description, isn't it boss?" The twinkle in Nick's eye brought a chuckle from Kendall. "On a serious note, you read my text last night?"

"Early this morning. Apparently all the pieces came together with good cooperation from the Feds. I know this one was personal, Nick. Have you spoken to Maureen?"

"Last night. She's agreed to tell all she knows about Santia, so it delays her return a day or so. But I'll survive. Got lots to keep me busy today with a bail hearing. By the time the judge reads my denial request, with all the evidence we've gotten, denial shouldn't be a problem."

Kendall added, "Judge Allen is a pretty tough bird. He knows this will be a high profile case and he's not going to take a chance on Wilson skipping town. I suppose he's got himself a high-priced lawyer."

"No doubt. I've been mulling something over, boss. Since Wilson is a member of the bar, knows the law inside and out, I believe an interrogation is a waste of time. He's not going to confess to Owen's murder or the fact that he's an accomplice to Judge Ramsey's death. His lawyer is going to have him plead the fifth every time I come at him with an incriminating question. What do you think?"

Kendall pursed his lips as he gave Nick's statement some thought. "You're probably right, but don't be surprised if they come back with a plea bargain on the Ramsey issue."

"You mean have Wilson turn on Santia, tell everything he knows for a lighter sentence?"

"That's usually what happens in these cases. Friendship takes a back seat when it comes down to the wire. Could be another interesting day, Nick. Keep me informed."

* * *

"Hey, great news you texted last night," called Connor as he caught sight of Nick unlocking his office. It sure is sweet when the good guys win one. Maureen coming home today?"

Nick pushed the door aside and motioned for Connor to follow him. "She's giving a deposition to the Feds, and I expect the SEC will want to talk to her too, seeing as she was a client with Worldwide. I expect her to make a reservation for tomorrow, but she'll let me know when to pick her up. Can't be too soon as far as I'm concerned. This whole thing's been surreal."

"The worst is over, pal." Connor gave Nick a pat on the shoulder. "Call if you need me."

After working on his written bail denial presentation for over an hour, Nick walked over to Connor's office and asked him to proof read it to be sure nothing was omitted.

"Looks good to me—death bed confession, matching tire tracks, bloody clothes. My bet is that Wilson's money's no good this time."

"Listen, cover this one for me, will you? Tim Graham, the FBI agent, asked me to fax everything we have on Santia, so I'm tied up. We don't want him on the loose with bail, either. Of course, the kidnapping charges should be enough to hold him, but I want the Feds to get their hands on our murder evidence as soon as possible."

"The SEC will want their piece of the pie, as well," added Connor. "Oh, what a tangled web we weave when first we practice to deceive."

Nick looked at his partner and quizzed, "That sounds like a line from my high school English class. Who penned it anyway? Sure nails Santia."

"Sir Walter Scott. But don't ask me to repeat another line because my memory stops there."

"No problem 'cause I can't stand around and listen to you spout poetry all day anyway. Back to earning a living, partner."

* * *

By lunchtime, Nick had assembled all reports, photos, prints, and a copy of the Walmart video to send to the Boston FBI headquarters. He needed a break and decided to drive out to the fish camp and check on Otis. Besides, his friend, busy with funeral arrangements for his brother, hadn't heard that Maureen was found safe.

Nick welcomed the fresh air tinted with a hint of Jasmine as he drove past garden after garden. He felt his body relax and he realized how tense the past few days had been. After several minutes, Lucky announced Nick's arrival before the Camaro came to a stop in the lane leading up to the cabin. The dog's barking brought Otis around the corner of the building carrying a garden hoe in his hand. He hurried over to Nick, "Did you find her, Nick? I worried all night over that gal."

"I found her all right—kidnapped. Santia flew her to Boston in his plane around noon yesterday."

A gasp erupted from Otis's throat. "How you know that?"

"Would you believe that little tip you gave me 'bout the guy hanging out across from the camp in the bay? Just didn't seem right. A true fisherman doesn't sit in one spot all day. Then I remembered Maureen mentioned he had a plane. I checked over at Milton Airport and two witnesses saw them fly away. I alerted the FBI in Boston and they picked him up at a small airport. I got the call about ten last night."

A worried expression crossed Otis's brow. "He didn't hurt her, did he, Nick?" The grip Otis held on the hoe handle tightened.

"Don't believe so. The Feds would have told me. She'll fly back tomorrow evening. I'm picking her up at the Pensacola airport at five-thirty."

Otis gave Nick a thoughtful look then spoke. "I know you're anxious to have Maureen to yourself, but this whole affair calls for a celebration. We's free, Miz Maureen and me." Otis's voice plead, "Bring her back down for a good ole fashioned fish fry. I gets my kin to bring the cornbread, beans, and coleslaw. And you know I gonna have all kinds of fish." Otis took a breath and continued, "Aunt Lucy never go to a gatherin' without her special red velvet cake. What you say, Nick? Welcome Miz Maureen home in style."

Nick saw the sparkle ignite in his friend's eyes. *How can I refuse?* He placed his hand on Otis's shoulder and said, "It would mean a lot to you, wouldn't it?"

"Yes, sir. Ain't no celebrations in prison. Bin a long time since I heard laughter and singin'. My people can harmonize like you never heard before."

"You convinced me—especially that part about the red velvet cake," laughed Nick.

A smile that revealed pearly-white teeth stretched from ear to ear as Otis chuckled, "You thinkin' of askin' Miz Maureen to marry you. Bout time!"

"Not yet, but I promise you we aren't leaving the airport until she says yes."

Otis turned his head upward and with tears running down his black cheeks, he called out, "Hallelujah! Mama, there gonna be a weddin' soon—be lookin' down, you hear?"

Chapter Thirty-Five

Nick's day began at 6:00 a.m. with the sun casting a warm glow over the horizon. Refreshed and eager to accomplish his lists of last-minute tasks for the evening ahead, he bounded out of bed and went straight for the shower. As the water pelted against his skin, he audibly recited the list he'd assembled the night before: call Peggy to clean the house and change the bed linens, stock the refrigerator with food and drinks, call the florist and order a bouquet, buy the ring, and—it occurred to him as he toweled his head dry—get a haircut.

Gonna be another busy day. I can see it coming. No doubt about that. Another thought crossed his mind and he remembered Owen's burial was set for this morning. He offered to go and support Otis, but the family asked for a private ceremony at the cemetery. No church service was planned. *Well, at least I got permission to remove Otis's ankle bracelet yesterday.*

"We gonna end the day on a positive note, Nick. The celebration we plannin' will help my family a lot."

Despite the day's agenda, to Nick, the hours dragged on. Connor teased, "If you don't stop looking at your watch, you're going to give yourself whiplash."

"Oh, sorry, hadn't realized I was showing my feelings. You're right. I guess I'm a little nervous. Don't know what I'll do if she turns me down."

"You and I know that's not going to happen, so let's finish this extradition paperwork on Santia." Connor laughed. "Wouldn't surprise me if a lynching gang took over the courthouse like in the old days the minute Santia crosses the Santa Rosa line. You know how the folks around this county felt about Judge Ramsey."

Nick looked at Connor and raised his eyebrows. "I hope you're not serious. You've been watching too many late night cowboy movies." But I have to admit, it's one trial I don't want to miss."

"Wilson's trial is going to get headlines, too. Thank goodness his bail was denied. According to the owner of that convenience store where I get my gas, the locals are already upset. They're saying you can't trust even the hometown officials anymore. Looks like they're right."

Nick finished off the last of his ham sandwich and tossed the wrapper into the trash can. "Shame isn't it? Rumor has it Wilson's attorney is already fishing around for a plea bargain. Of course, Sam's still going to stand trial for Owen's murder, so either way his goose is cooked."

At 4:30, Nick checked his watch for the last time and straightened up his desk in preparation to leave for the day. He slipped on his jacket and started out the door when his cell rang. *This better be important* he quipped to himself.

"Melino, here." A short pause followed until Nick, for the second time in four hours, recognized Graham's voice.

"Nick, are you able to talk?"

"Sure. I'm on my way to the airport to pick up Maureen, but I still have some time. No change of plans, I hope."

For the next ten minutes Nick listened to Graham's story and with each word he heard, the veins in his neck bulged and his face reddened. "Are you serious? This is bizarre—totally off the wall! I don't know what you did to get Santia to talk, including waterboarding, but I'm grateful for the tip."

Nick listened again as Graham brought the conversation to a close. "We're all on the same team, Melino."

Before the agent hung up, Nick got in the last word. "Hey, the next time you're down this way how 'bout a game of golf—on me? I owe you one. Later."

Without any hesitation Nick called Connor and sketched out Graham's message. "Get out to Santia's cabin ASAP. Call Judge Allen on your way and tell him you need immediate entry. Break in any way you can."

* * *

For the first time he could remember, Nick looked forward to driving to the Pensacola Airport, going around in circles looking for a parking space, waiting in a crowded welcoming area, and finally grabbing someone's luggage off the rotating carousel.

Nick reached inside his jacket left breast pocket and felt the contents. *Oh, yeah, she's going to be surprised.*

A Delta 707 touched down as he walked toward the main terminal. The arrival and departure screen indicated that Maureen's flight was on time. *Great! No waiting.*

Nick surveyed the welcoming crowd. Fortunately it was thin today. A mom with a crying baby in her arms and an energized toddler who kept running circles around his mother's legs kept repeating, "Daddy home soon. Daddy home soon."

Two teenage boys, tattooed from neck to ankle stood gyrating to whatever noise flowed into their earbuds. An elderly man sat in a wheelchair mesmerized by the commotion around him. Beside the escalators, two uniformed Santa Rosa County deputies tipped their hat at Nick as he moved to the front and center.

After a few minutes, passengers of all descriptions swarmed into the corridor like ants rushing toward a bread crumb. Nick's eyes scanned each female until only a handful of stragglers remained. In an instant, he recognized red hair dancing around a woman who set her gaze on him. Nick's smile broadened with each step she took in his direction. Once again, adrenaline swept through his body as she returned his greeting.

Six more steps took her into Nick's arms and she closed the gap between them. Her glistening lips begged for his so he readily obliged, then stepped back and handed his lady a bouquet of daisies.

"My favorite!" she squealed burying her face into the blossoms. You're just the sweetest guy welcoming me home with flowers."

A coy smile curled the edges of his lips as he crooned, "And I've got something else for you."

The woman in front of him danced with delight as her eyes followed his hand move into his jacket pocket. Nick took his time as he watched her anticipation grow. Then in one swift movement, he pulled out a pair of handcuffs and ordered her to put her hands behind her back.

Shock replaced ecstasy and she cried out, "Nick, it's me, Maureen. What's going on?"

"You tell me because you are not Maureen!"

"Of course I am. Who else would I be?"

Nick pushed back a portion of hair that dangled down from her left temple. "Nope. Not the Maureen I know. No mole. And here's another news flash—she's allergic to daisies. Won't touch them."

Without further adieu, Nick read her Miranda rights and the deputies walked to the scene and waited for their orders.

By now onlookers gathered around them and the last thing Nick wanted was interference.

"Take her to the patrol car, guys, and straight to booking."

Once settled into his Camaro, Nick shook his head as if to shake off the events of the last fifteen minutes. *Could this woman really be Maureen's twin? Why is Santia leaking this information? I've dealt with one set of troubled twins this past month, I don't need another. But the resemblance is uncanny—even her speech sounds like Maureen's with that Boston diction. Why is she involved with the likes of Santia?* Question after question invaded his thoughts. *An interrogation should shed some light on this strange turn of events, but right now my main concern is Maureen.*

As if willing his cell to ring with news from Connor, the familiar jingle actually startled him. He'd never heard Connor's voice so sober. "I'm at Santia's cabin, Nick. We found Maureen cuffed to a bed."

"What! Cuffed to a bed! Is she alive?" Nick felt as though he'd stopped breathing.

"Yes, but confused and fatigued. My guess is she was drugged with something that knocked her out."

"Get her to the hospital. I'm on my way."

Nick challenged the speed limit all the way down I-10 to the Milton exit. On Berryhill Road, he saw the Santa Rosa Medical Center parking lot entrance. He took an empty space near the emergency zone entrance, jumped out of the car, and ran up to the doors, as his eyes darted from side to side in search of Maureen.

He knew his way around this hospital, so in seconds he was in the emergency room. Connor, a nurse, and the E.R. doctor stood beside a bed with an open curtain. A mass of tangled red hair spread across the pillow and a face devoid of color looked up at Nick. The whites of her emerald eyes bore streaks of pink and the skin under her bottom eyelashes was swollen and dark. She reached for his hand and he squeezed her trembling fingers. The nurse began an IV for dehydration and the doctor pulled the privacy curtain as a hint for the men to leave and let him do an examination. Connor and Nick stepped back into the waiting room.

"Are you positive this imposter is Maureen's sister? asked Connor.

"We'll run a DNA on her, but my guess is they're siblings." Nick rubbed his chin, an old habit he acquired through the years when he puzzled over a problem." I don't understand why Maureen never mentioned she has a sister."

"Skeletons in the closet, I guess, partner. Everyone has one or two, don't you think? This whole Santia confession doesn't make any sense either. Why tell the Feds the woman on the plane with him is not who she says she is?"

"According to Graham, Santia would rat on his own mother if it meant saving his hide. He figured out pretty quickly that with the SEC closing in and now the FBI charging him with murder, he'd bring down anyone who knew more than they should. He claims Shannon, that's the name he gave her, worked for Worldwide luring wealthy business men to invest in the company. She was an insider, no doubt about that."

"But why come back to Milton to pose as your girlfriend?"

Nick looked at Connor and he lowered his voice. "I was next on their hit list. Santia told Graham they hatched a plan as they flew to Boston. First get rid of Maureen, then me. We both know too much. I'm convinced Shannon knows where to get her hands on a weapon—probably hidden in the cabin. My guess is that she's the one who drugged Maureen. I'll get it out of her tomorrow at her interrogation."

After half an hour, the emergency room door swung open and the nurse beckoned the men to come in. They gathered around Maureen's bed and the doctor gave them a reassuring smile as he explained, "Maureen is going to be fine. Lucky lady, though. Someone injected insulin into her veins. Too much of that drug could easily have stopped her heart."

Nick squeezed her hand and the love in his eyes spilled over in tears. "That's my fightin' Irish girl. Can she leave now, doc?"

"I recommended she stay for a twenty-four hour observation, but she insists she wants to leave. Since she's a medical examiner, I'll give her a green light. She knows her body and when it needs help." The doctor winked at his patient as he said, "Something tells me you'll be well taken care of. Drink lots of water and get enough rest."

Nick looked at the man's name tag, shook his hand, and thanked him for his promptness in examining Maureen.

Once in the parking lot, Connor gave Maureen a hug, and looked at Nick. "Okay, partner, see you in about an hour." With that he jogged over to his car.

Maureen tugged on Nick's sleeve. "What was that all about? Where are you going? Isn't it well past your work day?"

"You are going to be treated to the best Southern meal you could imagine, my dear. Otis and his family have planned a celebration at the fish camp and I couldn't turn him down. Actually, they think you were flown to Boston and are returning, as I did until my call from an FBI Agent Graham telling me this bizarre story. We have a lot of catching up to do, but first I have to ask one question. Do you have a twin sister named Shannon?"

Maureen's color drained from her cheeks. "Yes, but how do you know?"

"Let's get on the road and I'll tell you."

Chapter Thirty-Six

By the time Nick and Maureen reached the fish camp, each told their side of the events that transpired the past two days.

"Shannon and I never bonded as twins. She always wanted more and more attention and insisted my parents favored me over her. It wasn't that way at all. Because of her rebellious behavior, they had to use discipline. She resented it and left home as soon as she turned eighteen."

"Must have been hard on your parents. I'm so grateful my daughter hung in there with me after my divorce. She could have gone her own way, too."

"Can you imagine the shock I felt when Rod brought me to his cabin and there sat my sister calmly sipping a glass of wine on the front porch? She wasted no time in venting more of her venom. All the while, Rod's telling her to hurry and get it over with. I had no idea she would try to drug me to death. The next thing I know, I'm blindfolded, led into a bedroom, cuffed to the bed, and stuck with a needle. The rest is what you already know." By now Maureen's cheeks dripped tear after tear."

Nick reached over and laid his hand on her shoulder. "It's over, baby. No one is ever going to hurt you again. I promise." To change the mood, he let out a whoop! "Wow! Look at all Otis's kin."

Several little black boys ran around the yard chasing a soccer ball while the girls with a multitude of spiral ringlets all tied with colorful bows danced and played with Lucky. Their mamas scurried back and forth between the cabin and a long picnic table carrying bowls of one mouth watering recipe after another. In the center, a huge platter of golden-fried chicken and fish lured everyone to the feast.

The moment Otis spied Maureen, he wiped his hands on his apron and ran to give her his best hug. "Listen up, y'all. This beautiful lady is come home. We gonna thank the Lawd he take care of her. Now, bow you heads."

A hush came over the crowd until Aunt Lucy spoke up. "Now, Otis, the Lawd knows we's thankful, so don't take too long so's the food don't git cold. Miz Maureen probably hungry, too." A chorus of "amen" rose in unison.

After the blessing, everyone devoured the homemade salads, baked beans, bread, casseroles, pickles, and desserts. As the sun sank lower on the horizon and the moon rose higher, someone lit the fire pit, and one by one lawn chairs formed a circle around the glowing flames. A single soprano voice trilled the words of "Stand By Me" and as if on cue several others brought in the harmony. The emotion wrought by the song brought Maureen to tears and she clung to Nick.

One after another Negro spiritual melodies filled the night air until little babies and children were lulled to sleep. The fire died down and eventually only Otis, Maureen, and Nick peered into the embers.

Sensing it was time to leave his friends alone, Otis stood up and stretched his limbs. "Why, look at that moon. It way past my bedtime. Good night y'all."

Before he turned toward the cabin, Maureen jumped up and kissed him on the cheek. Thank you, my friend. This evening was exactly what I needed. Bless you."

"We both blessed, honey. You gonna spend the night?"

"I don't want to leave. Just one more night, okay?"

"Me too, Otis. I still have my sleeping bag in my car."

"Hey, no problem. There'll be fresh biscuits for breakfast. Night y'all."

Nick took Maureen's hand and started walking toward the bay. "Remember almost a year ago when we were at Connor and Heather's wedding, I told you that a local folk lore says if you walk on the beach in the moonlight and leave your footprints in the sand, you'll never leave Florida." Nick slid his arm around her waist and pulled her closer to him." Whether that's true or not, I never want you to leave Florida. I love you. Work was the only thing that kept me from losing my mind when you went missing."

Maureen raised her head and looked into his moonlit face. "I want to believe the legend is true because I have no intentions of leaving the man I love. That happens to be you, Nick Melino."

"Then that settles it."

"What do you mean?"

Nick's left hand gently raised her chin and his lips brushed against hers. "We have an appointment at the courthouse tomorrow."

"An appointment. For what?"

Another kiss lingered longer than the first. "To get our marriage license. Unfortunately, the State of Florida requires a three day waiting period before we can be married.

Bummer! In the meantime, there's no law that says you can't wear an engagement ring."

Nick stepped away and pulled a velvet oval box from his jacket pocket. As he opened the lid, a sliver of light from the moon caught one of the diamonds facets and its beauty caused Maureen to gasp.

With no hesitation, Nick simply asked, "Will you marry me?"

Maureen's answer was just as direct. "Yes, yes, a thousand times yes!"

With the ring on her finger, Nick embraced his fiancée and sealed the promise with a long and passionate kiss.

A chorus of mate-calling bullfrogs croaked their mantra as if giving their approval.

~The End~

About the Author

Sylvia Melvin lives in Milton, Florida. She is an Elementary Intervention teacher.

Her Canadian heritage is often reflected in her writing. She enjoys writing short stories, biographies, romance, and mysteries.

As one of the founding members of the Panhandle Writer's Group, she is motivated by her fellow writers and the skills she has learned.

Made in the USA
Charleston, SC
21 February 2015